The Unhanged Man

Also by Alan Hunter:
The Honfleur Decision
The Scottish Decision
Death on the Heath
Gently Between Tides
Death on the Broadlands

The Unhanged Man

Alan Hunter

Walker and Company
New York

All the characters and events portrayed in this story are fictitious.

First published in the United States of America in 1984 by the Walker Publishing Company, Inc.

Originally published in Great Britain in 1984 as *The Unhung Man* by Constable & Co., Ltd.

Library of Congress Cataloging in Publication Data

Hunter, Alan.
The unhanged man.

I. Title.
PR6015.U565U5 1984 823'.914 84-19493
ISBN 0-8027-5602-6

Printed in the United States of America

10 9 8 7 6 5 4 3 2 1

IN MEMORY OF A.A. ROUSE

who may or may not have been guilty, but who was unmercifully pursued by his accuser, and who was denied the benefit of clear medical grounds for a verdict of diminished responsibility. May we never see such trials again.

The characters and events in this book are fictitious; the locale is sketched from life.

1

Perhaps because it was a market day at Mazebridge and the High Street was bustling with stalls and vehicles, nobody especially noticed a woman standing, as though transfixed, on the pavement.

She had just come out of a milliner's shop and was carrying one of their trendy black bags. At a glance, you might have put her at thirty, but then you would notice the wrinkles at the corners of her eyes. She was well-dressed. She wore a sheepskin coat over a lamb's-wool jumper and a pleated plaid skirt. And her eyes had gone wide, like a cat's: she was staring at a man on the opposite pavement.

It was March, the first day of spring, though you might easily have taken it for May. The wind had gone south and was chasing brilliant cumulus clouds across a sky of fire blue. On the downs outside the town foolish hares were indulging in boxing and wrestling matches, lambs were bleating among the tumuli and the White Horse galloped boldly in the freshening grass. Here in the High Street there was a special flavour, a richer quality of light and shade; winter had gone. Sounds, too, were more echoey, seeming to match the enhanced brilliancy of colours.

At first, the man didn't notice the woman. He was a farmer, that was apparent. A tall, hard-framed man of fifty or so, he wore breeches thrust into green derriboots. He was walking as though in thought, hands in pockets, pushing past people; his tanned, large-featured face a little drooped, his wiry, greying hair uncovered. A sad face. Somehow one got the impression of a solitary man, a widower no doubt. Yet there was energy about him too.

Then it was as though the stare of the woman somehow

penetrated the consciousness of the man: his head jerked up and he looked around him, his eyes drawn suddenly to hers. And he, too, stood as though transfixed, his eyes large and disbelieving: it may have been for several seconds that they gazed at each other across Mazebridge High Street.

Finally he took advantage of a gap in the traffic to dodge across to where she stood. Yet still he hesitated uncertainly, eyes ready for a rebuff.

'Is it . . . can it be?'

Her eyes now smiling, she nodded.

'Good God! And after how many years?'

'Too many for me. But you've scarcely changed.'

He seemed dazed. He brushed a hand across his hair, made to speak and then didn't. Meanwhile they were being buffeted by passers-by, women with shopping-baskets, men laden with parcels.

'Look . . . can't we go somewhere?'

'I was about to go for coffee.'

Of the two she had much more self-possession, had already taken a grip of the encounter.

'You know it's ridiculous, but since I got back you're the first person I've met who used to know me.'

'Have you been back long?'

'Two years.'

'What are you doing in Mazebridge?'

'I farm near here.'

She touched his elbow, and together they strolled along the busy pavement. Coffee was being served in the lounge of the Red Lion and they found a booth and sat down opposite each other. He was hungrily scanning her smooth face with its snub nose and shapely mouth; his eyes had a wildness in them. She held herself smiling for his inspection.

'Oh lord. You haven't changed a bit. You're still the girl I knew at Prior's.'

'What nonsense. I have a grown-up son. But tell me what you're doing in England.'

He made a gesture of frustration. 'I'm damned if I know. It

seemed a good idea at the time. But it isn't working. I've lost my roots. I'll probably drift back to Africa again.'

'Haven't you a family?'

His mouth was sardonic. 'I married a girl from S.A. . . . She went back there. Now she's married to a college professor with a Dutch name. She took the kids with her, a girl and a boy, and they're grown up and the girl's married. The boy's in the S.A. civil service. End of story about my marriage.'

'But your own people?'

'Father's dead. Mother lives with my sister in Jo'burg.'

'And you came back here?'

'I'm English, aren't I? At least, I was before I went out.'

His voice was surprising, soft, cultivated, quite different from that of the average farmer. But it wasn't quite English any longer, had a faint slur in the vowel sounds.

'You went out there young.'

'Too young. I should have married you before I went.'

'Why didn't you write?'

'There seemed no point. I'd cut my roots and had to start afresh.'

'I often wondered about you.'

He nodded. 'But you were in Europe, I was there. A new world, new people, and the estate kept us grafting. Then I met this girl down in Cape Town who'd got relatives she visited in Salisbury, and from that she got to staying with us, and about that time father bought the farm next door. It was good going in those days. I never expected to come back. But then everything fell apart and I was alone in a bit of black Africa.'

'Was there trouble, then?'

'No trouble. Unless it was the trouble inside me.'

He drank nervously, retaining the cup, his eyes avoiding hers. In spite of the greying hair, the lined features, there was a boyish touch in his appearance. He was wearing an open-necked shirt and a tweed jacket, neither new.

'And you?'

'Oh, me. Well, I'm on my second husband.'

'How's that?'

'I lost my first in a car smash some years ago.'

He didn't know quite what to reply to that.

'My second is an old family friend,' she smiled. 'He's ancient, but we're good company, and I was left on my own like you. Stephen, that's my son, is practising law in Hong Kong. So I hitched up with Arthur, and it's worked out very well.'

'And you love him?'

'Let's talk about you. What's so wrong with farming in England?'

He stared at her for a while before replying: 'It's me, I guess. Not England.'

'That's silly.'

He shook his head. 'I don't belong here any more. I don't belong in Zimbabwe either, it was Rhodesia when I went there. My roots are all cut, I'm a bloody wandering Jew. I live alone in a big farmhouse with a woman coming in to cook and tidy. I've got an offer from a pal down in the Congo to run an agency up-country and I'll probably take it, drift back there, become Bwana of the River. Then I'll go crazed a bit, there'll be black girls, whisky for breakfast, lunch and tiffin, then some horrible bloody disease and a witch-doctor chanting me out. *Un déraciné*. You wouldn't know.'

In his eyes was the wild look again, and he was perspiring. It was certainly strange-sounding talk for the lounge of the Red Lion.

'You don't believe that, really.'

'I try. I keep trying.'

'You haven't given yourself a chance here.'

'The farm doesn't pay. I don't break even.'

'Listen. Somehow I feel responsible for you.'

'Why should you feel responsible for me?'

'I don't know . . . old times. I used to feel responsible for you then. And you need a friend, that's plain, someone you used to know before, a root you didn't cut. You can belong here again.'

He stared hard. 'You're crazy.'

'No. I'm talking sound sense. We've got to get you back on the rails. You're not really such an outcast as you pretend.'

'I'm a lost cause, me. Better let me go to the devil.'

'No.'

He kept staring, struck by the firmness in her plangent voice.

Around them farmers were gossiping and laughing, and farmers' wives, sturdy and complacent, while through the window one saw floats passing, some with cattle peering over the tailboard. The man had a name. No matter. The woman had a name. No matter. Not on that breezy day in March when the blackthorn was snowing the lanes, the hares courting, the wheatears creaking and the White Horse galloping over his downs.

Mazebridge, Wilts., admin. centre, mkt. town (Sat.), E.C. Thurs., Pop. 5,651, The Red Lion ★★★.

But then it was a morning in May, also breezy, also with a round, rippling sun, and Gently was passing through the pegged-back swing doors of New Scotland Yard into the bustle of reception. From all of which his mind was distant: he was fresh back from a weekend at Heatherings. What was walking through the swing doors with him was a memory of gorse and of hawthorns in Proustian splendour.

For that had been the weekend when the gorse was at its height on the heaths around Heatherings. In a little winding valley close to the house it had been glowing with a brilliance that almost made one flinch. Could even darkness have drowned such colour? He and Gabrielle had gone wandering there in a trance, down to a little thicket at the end of the valley where, unbelievably, they were greeted by a nightingale. Not a shy nightingale, either, but one that perched on a scrub-oak to return their inspection. Then, on a lilac growing wild in the thicket, they had come upon six Green Hairstreak butterflies.

A dream to carry back to London, to the flat in Lime Walk, alone: since Gabrielle was staying on at Heatherings to hang new curtains, with Mrs Jarvis. A dream that made London seem a prison and the greens of the town trees artificial; along with the sadness of missing Gabrielle. Without her, the emptiness of the flat seemed a presence.

'Sir—sir!'

He came out of his vision to find a messenger tagging beside him.

'Sir, the Assistant Commissioner wants to see you first thing, says not to wait for morning conference.'

Gently grunted. 'What's come in?'

'Don't know, sir. Nothing we've heard about.'

But it had to be something of importance for Gently to be paged in this fashion. Getting out of the lift, he went first to his office, where he found Dutt chatting with one of the D.C.s.

'What's on the grapevine?'

But Dutt couldn't tell him, nor could Blondie, the A.C.'s secretary. All she knew was that there'd been some closed-door sessions and that the A.C. had spent most of Sunday at the Yard. Mysteriouser and mysteriouser! And to cap it all, the A.C. was waiting at the door of his office: an event unknown. In the usual way, one tapped and awaited his imperial leisure.

'Get inside, Gently.'

He was well-nigh furtive, pausing to look up and down the corridor. Then he closed the door himself, and Gently could hear the snick of the bolt.

'Now listen. Just how discreet are you?'

That didn't seem to require an answer. After a moment, Gently took out his pipe and stuck it empty between his teeth.

'Oh, sit down, damn you.'

Never had he known the A.C. to be so much on edge.

'What I'm going to tell you now is known by only five men, and one of those is the Home Secretary.'

'The Home Secretary?'

'That's what I said! The Commissioner and your colleague Pagram are two others. Something has occurred that you may dream about in nightmares, but which you pray will never happen while you're in charge. Well, it has. And your capable hands have been elected to carry the can.'

'Is this political?'

'Not political, though it may have political repercussions. In fact that may well be the outcome if word of it ever leaks to the press.'

The A.C. was speaking with lowered voice and leaning across his desk towards Gently. Perhaps just because he was being so conspiratorial, Gently was finding it hard to take him seriously. Yet the A.C. himself appeared deadly serious: the eyes behind his glasses were unwinking.

'Do you read the papers?'

'Well—yes.'

'There was a filler paragraph in two of them. A shooting accident in Wiltshire. A former judge, Arthur Pewsey.'

'The hanging judge?'

'Right. He is said to have hung forty men. He was found in a summerhouse in the grounds of his house, shot in the chest, with his own shotgun beside him.'

'A suicide?'

'They say it's unlikely—too far to stretch for the trigger. But an accident is possible, the fellow grounding his gun, letting it slip, strike the floor and jolt the hammer. But that's by the way. What the locals found was that the gun had probably been wiped, though Pewsey's hand was still curled round it and his prints were on the barrel. It made them jumpy, so they cast around and came up with a farmworker called Hinton, a man Pewsey had done a couple of times for ferreting on his property. There were signs that Hinton had been back there lately and the rabbit warren wasn't far from the summerhouse, so they hauled him in and he admitted having been there but says he cleared off after hearing the shot.'

'Has he been charged?'

'For the moment just listen! One mystery was what Pewsey was doing at the summerhouse. He had set out earlier that afternoon to attend a meeting of the Local Magistrates' Association in Mazebridge. The meeting began at three-thirty but Pewsey left his house at two, and his car was found pulled off a minor road running along a boundary of his estate—a road that further on passes the warren, and also Hinton's cottage.'

‘Could he have been laying for Hinton?’

‘Perhaps. But the locals have a different theory. It seems that Pewsey had been making war on the grey squirrels that were infesting his woods—hence the gun. Apparently the house is backed by woodland that used to harbour red squirrel, and when the greys began to drive them out Pewsey took to carrying a gun. So the locals’ theory is that, having an hour to spare, Pewsey drove round to the back of his woods, intending to blast a few squirrels, and there caught Hinton red-handed.’ The A.C. sniffed. ‘Did you ever meet Pewsey?’

‘Once or twice I gave evidence before him.’

‘Then you will know he was a tough old buzzard and as spry as a spider. I can well imagine him tackling a poacher and marching him off at gunpoint—to lock him up in the summer-house, the locals think, while he went to ring the police. But Hinton had a suspended sentence hanging over him after his second prosecution, so he was desperate, there was a struggle and the gun went off, killing Pewsey. And to answer your question, no, they haven’t charged Hinton, but they think they have a case. And so they would have—but for one thing.’ The A.C. broke off to stare fiercely at a file that was lying on the desk. ‘Being a damned conscientious lot, they combed the summerhouse for dabs. They found a stranger-dab on the door knob that didn’t belong to any of the principals. It wasn’t on record with them and it wasn’t on record with us, either. But then Barnes the Twist got his interfering hands on it.’

‘Barnes . . .’

‘Yes, Gently.’

Gently could only stare back blankly. Barnes, always known as ‘the Twist’ because of an eccentric theory of his, was an elderly civilian who held a supernumerary post in Fingerprints. His theory was that a certain whorl-pattern occurred most frequently in the prints of violent criminals, with an incidence as high as one in three in those of convicted murderers. In pursuing this theory, over the years, he had formed a ‘Black Index’ of the prints of murderers. The theory was not taken seriously: Barnes was classed as a harmless crackpot.

'This print had the twist?'

'If only that were all! But Barnes went hunting through his bloody index. And he found a ringer. It was the thumbprint of a man who was hung at Crampton in '64. The man's name was Eric Cleeve, and Pewsey was the judge who sent him down.'

What could one say? Across the desk, he and the A.C. stared at each other. Then the A.C. opened the file before him and handed a document to Gently. It was the photostat of a doctor's case card, an untidy scribble, perhaps made at the slab. It read:

> Cleeve, Eric Trevor, 29. Judicial Hanging. Spine dislocated between the fourth and fifth cervical vertebrae, much displacement backward between sixth and seventh vertebrae, injuries to Brain and Spinal Cord. Exterior: well nourished. Ht. 5ft. 11¾in. Wt. 168lb. Drop 5ft. 11in. Dr. E. Rybury, M.O. H.M.P. Crampton. 19/2/64

The A.C. took the document back.

'Well?'

'He must surely have been dead enough,' Gently murmured.

'Indeed one would have thought so. But then how does he come to be leaving a thumbprint, eighteen years later?'

'Are we certain of the match?'

'Yes, Gently. Quite certain. Don't think we haven't double-checked it during the past forty-eight hours.'

'Could the print have been duplicated?'

'Why, how and by whom? Who could suppose it would ever be matched? If it hadn't been for Barnes, Cleeve's dabs would have been destroyed in '64.'

'Then . . . a coincidence?'

The A.C. snorted. 'The Home Secretary was pinning his hopes on that one. But we had to point out to him that it would be the first example in the whole history of fingerprinting, the world over. No. The dab on the door knob was Cleeve's, and don't tell me that it had been sitting there for eighteen years. It was fresh. The summerhouse had been entered by Mrs Pewsey the day before. So Cleeve was hung, but Cleeve is alive, vertebrae, brain injury, quicklime and all. And if he is alive, then he had the motive to shoot Judge Pewsey. Do you remember the trial?'

'Not in detail.'

'It happens that I remember it very well. Cleeve was tried at Lewes, near my little place, so I took more than a passing interest in it.'

The A.C.'s 'little place', as Gently chanced to know, was an Elizabethan manor house in Ashdown Forest, from which he commuted most of the week in a maroon Bentley, driven by himself.

'Cleeve was a claims clerk at the Brighton branch of Southern Alliance Insurance. His boss was found battered to death in his office and the safe had been tampered with. The caretaker remembered that Cleeve had been working late and Cleeve had no alibi for that evening; he was in debt, and a bloodstained jemmy was found in a dustbin outside his flat. In court Cleeve made a good impression, while his defence stressed how heavily the prosecution was depending on their principal witness, the caretaker; but Pewsey's summing up was vindictive and he virtually dictated a Guilty verdict. It was clearly perverse, and everyone expected it to be overturned on appeal. But the appeal court held that the summing up, though strong, was not unfair, and in the absence of fresh evidence or a point of law, upheld the verdict. So Cleeve was topped a week later, protesting innocence to the last.' The A.C. paused. 'Not, perhaps, a testimonial to British Justice. But you get an impression from a lot of those hanging trials that it was the example and not the fine print that mattered.'

Gently sucked his empty pipe. 'Then if Cleeve is still alive . . .'

'Precisely.' Involuntarily, the A.C. glanced over his shoulder before leaning forward still closer to Gently. 'So you can see why the Home Secretary is passing blue lights. This could be Timothy Evans in reverse. The media would have hysterics and the Opposition be howling for blood. Luckily Barnes came to me with it so I was able to sit on him. Then I discussed it with the Commissioner, and we took it straightway to the H.S. As a result, Pagram has been to Crampton and made enquiries here and there. Up to now we have nothing positive. But there's a smell about it, Gently.'

Gently sucked a little more. 'Anything irregular would have needed the connivance of at least six men.'

'Five, as it happened,' the A.C. nodded. 'Which is where it begins to smell. Regulations called for six men to be present.' He began counting them off on his fingers. 'The prison governor, the prison chaplain, the prison medical officer, the hangman, and the two warders who attended the prisoner in the death cell. But one of the warders wasn't present. He was let off by the governor. And by a lucky chance he is still at Crampton, and Pagram was able to talk to him. It seems there was trouble in the death cell when the hangman went to pinion Cleeve, everyone was upset and this warder, a youngish man, was told to go home. Pagram said the man didn't want to talk about it, he had had nightmares ever since, but he did notice something as he was crossing the prison yard: a black van, which he took to be the hangman's, parked close to the door leading to the drop. It was backed up close to the door and had one of its own rear doors open. Could be something, could be nothing, but we're looking at anything a little unusual.'

Gently said: 'There would be a burial detail.'

'Yes. And Pagram talked to one of them. They were summoned to collect the body about three hours after the execution. That was normal. It was about the time needed for the doctor to do his PM, after which it was the hangman's duty to sew the body up in hessian.'

'So there was a body.'

'Oh yes. At least, something was waiting there on a bier.'

'Good enough to fool them.'

The A.C. shrugged. 'I don't suppose they inspected it any too closely. And the inquest appears to have been purely nominal, with the Coroner rubber-stamping Rybury's report. But here we get the smell again. There should be records and a plan of prison burials. They're missing at Crampton, and Pagram's informant couldn't remember the situation of the grave.'

'Records would be the governor's responsibility.'

'I am coming to the governor, Gently. Clearly if what we have here is a conspiracy, then the governor must have been at the centre of it. He was an interesting man. His name was Mathieson, and he came here from Canada in 1918. He was a Canadian Army conscript, and after the war he stayed in England and joined the prison service. He was appointed governor of Crampton in 1955 and retired ten years later. He died in 1977. And in private he was known to be an enthusiastic abolitionist. That's what we know about Henry Mathieson, and it doesn't make the Home Secretary any the happier.'

Gently kept slowly sucking. 'And the others?'

'You've seen the case card Rybury showed Pagram. Rybury is retired and lives in Bath, and swears there was nothing irregular about the execution. Same with the second warder, Eastcott, who retired at the same time as the governor. The chaplain, a Reverend Bassett, is presently running a mission school in Ghana. The hangman was Alfred Highway, and no doubt you remember what happened to him.'

Gently did. Alfred Highway had been found dead in mysterious circumstances—a hit-and-run accident, perhaps, but the weapon not necessarily a car.

'So then,' the A.C. resumed. 'Now you know the situation, Gently. Pagram will continue his probe at the Crampton end, you're to go down to Mazebridge and to liaise with the natives. Chief Detective Inspector Pypard is your man there, and him you may have to take into your confidence. Otherwise the man you are hunting is simply an ex-criminal who may have been out of the country for a time.'

Gently stared at the file. 'What exactly is wanted?'

'That is what I am about to tell you.' The A.C. darted a guilty look at the door, then sank his voice yet lower. 'That poacher fellow has his neck stuck out. I'm not asking you to fit him up.

But if you find there is case that the Public Prosecutor will look at, it would be a lucky break for everyone.'

'And if I don't?'

'Then these are your instructions. If Cleeve is the man we shall have to have him. But unless there's an open-and-shut case, needing no reference to motive, put him on a holding charge only.'

After a pause, Gently said: 'And then?'

'Not your decision. Nor mine either.'

'I was simply wondering . . .'

'Stop right there, Gently.'

Gently chewed on his pipe. Then he rose.

Back in his office, he opened the file and stared long at the two photographs of Cleeve contained in it. They showed a fresh-faced man with full cheeks and a plentiful mop of slightly-curled hair; and large, scared brown eyes that seemed already to be staring at the gallows. Add eighteen years . . .? Cleeve now would be forty-seven, his hair less plentiful and perhaps greying; the cheeks paler, eyes heavier-lidded, a certain slackness in every feature. A moustache, a beard might have been added, not to mention a wig and coloured contact lenses: even cosmetic surgery. The only sure thing about him was the ridges on the tips of his fingers. And this Cleeve didn't know: he would take few precautions about leaving fingerprints around. He was a dead man, off the record, must be feeling quite confident of his security. So would his confidence trap him? Oddly, for an instant, Gently seemed to feel a twitch of contact with this improbable man.

On an off-chance he rang Pagram's office and had the luck to catch him.

'I've just been briefed on you know what. Has anything fresh come in?'

One thing only: Pagram had discovered that Cleeve had had a twin brother.

'Probably the reddest of herrings, old man, but I'll do my best to run him down. Take it from me that there's nothing in the notion that identical twins have identical dabs.'

'Just thinking aloud, but if you had a hot property, where might it occur to you to hide it?'

'Aha.' Pagram hung on. 'And me sporting a maple leaf, you mean?'

'He had to be somewhere for eighteen years.'

'Ye-es,' Pagram said. 'I like it. Leave it with me.'

Gently hung up and at last got round to lighting his pipe.

2

Mazebridge involved a trip down the M4, but traffic that morning was happily light, and so it was not long after noon when Gently coasted into the small town. First impressions were agreeable. Mazebridge was a regular stone-belt town, watched over by a dumpy spire and backed by a line of green downs to the south. Georgian touches were plentiful in the High Street, where even the traffic seemed to loiter, and where a baroque coaching inn, the Red Lion, yawned its great archway on a paved yard. A timeless place: perhaps it was the yellow stone in which it was built that measured its hours out so slowly.

But the Police Station was in a side street and in small accord with what had preceded it. A smallish, modern building, it had an air of drab utility. Gently parked with difficulty in a crowded forecourt and ascended concrete steps to reception. There he was nearly bowled over by a solid, dark-haired man who had come bounding out of an office.

'Oof—sorry, sir! I'm Pypard. We didn't expect to see you so soon.'

He had a twinkling dark eye and grabbed Gently's hand energetically. The interior of the building was as drab as the exterior, boxy and low-ceilinged, with a lino-topped counter behind which a sergeant and two uniform-men stopped what they were doing to stare at the newcomer. Besides twinkling, Pypard's eyes were sly.

'We were a bit surprised, sir, by all this. Never thought that our little old job out here—'

'Shall we go to your office?'

'Of course. This way, sir.'

The office somehow suited the man: cluttered, untidy, yet

cheerful. Shelves bulged with box-files, papers littered the desk, and the door of a steel cabinet hung open. It smelled of tobacco-smoke; two empty cups stood beside a stacked ashtray. A younger man, hefty, fair-haired, rose as they entered.

'Detective Inspector Canning, sir. He's i/c of the case.'

Canning also took Gently's hand, but his attitude was more defensive. There were only two chairs so Canning remained standing; Pypard yielded the desk-chair to Gently.

'Some coffee, sir?'

'Not for the moment. First I would like you to fill me in on the case.'

'Well—yes, sir. But I don't know yet if it is a case, at least not one that would interest the Yard.'

Again the slyness in Pypard's eyes!

'You see, it's this way. We can't feel certain that Hinton did it. He could have, he admits being there, and he's come up with a cock-and-bull story since. But just as well it could have been an accident with the old boy banging down his gun, and one way or another we don't fancy bringing a charge. So if it's about anything at all it's about that dab we sent to the Yard. And that's a funny old thing to build a case on, with no one knowing whose it is.'

Now his eyes were sharp as needles, and Canning was watching Gently too. Doubtless they had been discussing just this when Gently's early arrival had surprised them. Had something been let slip in the message they would have received from the Yard? A little old country job . . . with just a dab making the difference.

Deliberately Gently lit his pipe and buried the match in the overflowing ashtray.

'Now listen carefully! I won't pretend this isn't a case of special interest. Judge Pewsey was a well-known person and we want to clear up any doubts about his death. At the same time we want to keep it discreet, with no word to the press about the Yard being here. If, as you think, the Judge's death was accidental, then there's a double reason for discretion. Is that understood?'

'Understood, sir. But at the same time we can't help wondering . . .'

'A case of special interest is what I said. We'll come back to that later.'

Gently puffed. Pypard dropped his eyes. He was far from satisfied, his expression said; but it was Gently's show, and it was up to him if that was the way he wanted to run it . . . Then his glance was shrewd.

'Perhaps you can tell us, sir, if we ought to regard it as a case of murder?'

'That is what I am here to find out. So the sooner you fill me in the better.'

'I just thought I'd raise the point, sir, because of this tale Hinton came up with. After we had sweated him a few times he gave us a line about another man.'

'Another man?'

'So he says, sir. Swore he saw one coming out of the summerhouse. Then he heard a car starting up and saw it driven away towards Clyffe.'

'Have you followed this up?'

Pypard's eyes were quirkish. 'So someone had to leave that dab, sir. But we haven't found a witness yet who can confirm Hinton's tale.'

And he himself, his tone said, didn't believe it, put it down as the invention of a clumsy liar. But if Gently cared to swallow it . . . He caught Gently's flat stare, and his expression became blank.

'I think I'll have that coffee after all.'

'Yes, sir. It is close to lunchtime.'

'Perhaps you'll arrange to have a snack brought in. And in the meantime, fetch me a map.'

Five minutes later they were sipping coffee and an Ordnance Survey map was spread over the desk. Pewsey had lived at the village of Erchildown, four miles from Mazebridge on the Prior's Compton road. The house, Erchildown New Place, stood in large grounds about half a mile beyond the village; it was backed by a high, circling, wooded ridge over which ran a footpath to the famous summerhouse. A minor road skirted the grounds and led to the village of Clyffe; one could see where it passed by the warren and then by Hinton's cottage. From it a lane entered Pewsey's property, leading to ruins marked as Erchildown Old Place. Summerhouse, warren and ruins appeared to be within hailing distance of each other.

'Show me where Pewsey's car was found.'

Pypard pointed to a spot beside the minor road. They had found it shoved into a gap among trees, invisible from the road until one came abreast of it.

'Any reason why he wouldn't have parked in that lane?'

Pypard looked at Canning, who shook his head. The spot indicated by Pypard could have been only a hundred yards short of the lane.

'Perhaps that was just where he wanted to be, sir,' Canning said. 'Him going in there after the squirrels. I saw plenty about when I was there, he wouldn't even have to have left the car.'

'But do we know for certain he was after squirrels?'

'Why else would he have taken the gun with him, sir?'

Gently shrugged. 'That's what I'm wondering.'

He caught Pypard looking towards the ceiling.

'It was a pretty regular thing, sir,' Canning said. 'He was out with his gun almost every day. His housekeeper heard the shot but paid no attention, even though she knew that the Judge had gone out. It was so usual.'

'She heard it from the house?'

'Yes, sir. Gives the time at about two-forty.'

'Who else was in the house?'

'Just Mrs Pewsey, sir. But she was lying down and didn't hear it.'

'Who else heard it?'

'Well, Hinton, sir. He gives the time about the same.'

Gently sipped some vile coffee, still pondering over the map. The summerhouse, the lane, the warren formed a little triangle, the figure of a drama still largely opaque. But the locals' appraisal probably held water, and Pewsey's entry on the scene was quite explicable . . . setting aside for the moment a ghost that had risen from the quicklime in a prison yard.

'You will have questioned Mrs Pewsey about her husband's state of mind.'

'She was quite emphatic, sir,' Canning said. 'The evening before, he was planning a cruise with some friends they had in. The Monktons, sir, they're local people with a good deal of clout, a yacht in the Med and all that. They were planning a cruise for next month. I had a word with Mr Monkton, who says the judge was quite his usual self.'

'He was a man who may well have made enemies.'

'Yes, sir. I hinted that to Mrs Pewsey. But she says no, she knew of nothing of that sort. And the Judge had been retired for three years.'

'He had prosecuted Hinton.'

'Well there you are, sir.' Canning stared, and let it die.

'Now let's have a run down of the facts.'

'Yes, sir.'

One was conscious of an increasing resentfulness about Canning. A youngish man, not much over thirty, he probably hadn't held his rank for long. Pypard, on the other hand, was more cagey: you felt he had learned to roll with the punches.

'It seems that the Judge set out at 2 p.m. on Friday, sir, driving his wife's car, a green Lancia, with the intention of attending this meeting of the Magistrates' Association at the Red Lion here. His wife was expecting him back for tea and when he didn't arrive she rang an acquaintance who had been at the meeting, then she mentioned the matter to the housekeeper, who remembered hearing a shot fired up in the woods. This alarmed Mrs Pewsey, and she sent the chauffeur-handyman to take a look round. He found the Judge in the summerhouse, with the door, which is usually kept locked, ajar. Then Mrs Pewsey rang us, the call being timed at 18.15 hours.'

'This chauffeur-handyman, where had he been earlier?'

'Name of Alton, sir. He's the housekeeper's husband. He

had been in town getting the weekend supplies, arrived back at the house at four p.m.'

'What other staff are there?'

'Just a maid living in, sir. It was her afternoon off and she was out with a boyfriend. Then there are two women who come in from the village, but they only come mornings. And a gardener four days a week, only Friday wasn't one of them. The Judge's tenant at the Home Farm looks after the rest of the grounds for him.'

'So Friday is the one afternoon when the house and grounds might be deserted.'

Canning looked blank. 'Well yes, sir. That's the way it works out.'

'In fact the time most likely for a confidential meeting, if the Judge had happened to have that in mind.'

'Yes, sir. If you say so. But we've found no evidence of it yet.'

'Carry on.'

Canning had coloured slightly. He threw a glance at Pypard, who avoided his eyes.

'We went out there, sir. The car was missing, but we soon found that. He had left it unlocked, with the door not closed properly, which suggested he might have left it in a hurry.'

'From the car, would he have had a view of the road?'

'He could have seen a bit of it, towards Clyffe.'

'As far as the warren?'

'I shouldn't think so, sir.'

'What about the lane?'

'He might perhaps have seen that.'

'Did you look for his tracks?'

'Well . . . not really, sir! It's hard ground there, with a lot of bracken. We took it he went through the woods and came out somewhere near the summerhouse. You can see the warren from the summerhouse, or a corner of it. He could have spotted Hinton from there.'

'Get on to what you found at the summerhouse.'

'Yes, sir.' Canning had turned a little pinker. 'We found the

Judge lying on the floor, a few feet from the door, sprawled out on his back with the gun still in his hand.'

Pypard produced photographs. They showed Pewsey, surprisingly, clad in a tweed plus-four suit, spreadeagled like a specimen, a dark mess staining the tattered breast of a waistcoat. The face Gently remembered, narrow, sunken, with a hooked nose and heavy brows; glassy eyes were open and staring, thin, colourless lips sagging. The last time he had seen that face it had been framed by a full wig. Now it looked shrunken and outraged: one could see that Pewsey had been almost bald.

'Had he money on him?'

'Yes, sir. Three hundred quid, mostly in tenners. Then there was a gold Longines watch that must have been worth over a thou.'

'How many cartridges did you find in his pockets?'

'None, sir.'

'Any in the car?'

Canning shook his head. There had been just the two in the gun, one expended, one not.

They produced the gun. It was a handsome twelve-bore but not a new pattern, an English make with a pistol-grip butt and hammers that stuck up like rabbit's ears. Pypard demonstrated how, when a hammer was cocked, a light bump to the butt was sufficient to discharge it. Accident was credible; and the force of the discharge might have thrown Pewsey backwards, just as found.

'But you found signs of its having been wiped?'

'Can't be certain of that, sir.' Pypard fondled the gun admiringly. 'All we can really say for certain is that the only dabs were where his hand was.'

'Dabs clear and unsmeared?'

'It could have happened, sir. If he'd been carrying the gun under his arm.'

'He lets it slip through his hand, the gun discharges and kills him, and still we are left with a clear set of dabs?'

'He could have gripped it as he fell, sir.'

Gently let it go. The car also had yielded nothing unexpected—the dabs of the dead man, his wife and his chauffeur, the former overlying the two latter.

'Now let's hear about the Hinton connection.'

'It was this way, sir,' Canning said gruffly. 'At first it looked like suicide, but then we talked to Mrs Pewsey and tried to reconstruct it with the gun.'

Another demonstration from Pypard—with the muzzle pressed to his chest, he could barely touch a trigger with his middle finger; and Pypard was five foot eleven, Pewsey a mere five seven and a half.

'So then we conducted a search of the scene, sir, and found Hinton's trademarks in the warren, the holes where he'd pegged his nets and his footprints in the sand. We guessed who it was and pulled him in, though at first he tried to deny it, then when we matched the tread on his wellies with the footprints he swore it was the day before when he'd been there. But that wouldn't wash either, sir, because there'd been rain overnight and the footprints were fresh. We had him cold, and in the end he admitted having been there and having heard the shot.'

'The same shot, the same time.'

'Yes, sir. He said he went in there at about twenty-five past two. He had got his nets down and was putting in the ferret when he heard the shot—says the ferret bit him, sir.'

'That much he could prove, sir,' Pypard grinned. 'He had his hand in a bandage when we pulled him. But whether it happened because of the shot is what the ferret isn't saying.'

Gently didn't smile. 'What else did Hinton say?'

'Says he laid low for a while, sir. We got it out of him that he wasn't expecting to run into the Judge because he knew about the meeting at the Red Lion—it seems that the maid's boyfriend is Hinton's eldest, and that's how he got his information. So he laid low for a while listening, then he lifted his nets and cleared out.'

'He heard the shot—but nothing else.'

'That was his first version, sir. But after we'd had a few more goes at him he perhaps decided that it wasn't enough.'

'You had been putting it to him that he shot the Judge.'

'Yes, sir,' Canning said flatly. 'I put it to him. So then he came up with version number two, about another man who drove off in a car.'

Pypard stirred. 'I was sitting in on this, sir, and my opinion is that Hinton was lying. There wasn't any man nor there wasn't any car. It was all a tale to get him off the hook.'

'Yet someone left a dab, as you pointed out.'

'Yes, sir. But with respect, we don't know when, sir.' Pypard's look was sly again, and he clearly had a point that he thought would be telling.

'Go on.'

'Well, it's like this, sir. That dab was on the inside knob of the door. And when people are using a summerhouse, how often do they close the door after them? So that dab may have been fresh or it may have been there for days.' His eyes tightened on Gently's. 'Unless there is any special reason, sir, why we have to assume it got there on Friday.'

Gently puffed. 'Meanwhile, we have a witness who claims to have seen a man there.'

'Oh yes, sir. For what it's worth.'

'Then perhaps we can hear exactly what he said.'

Pypard bowed his head, but he had the expression of a man who thinks he has scored. Canning shifted his feet slightly, his raw-boned features telling nothing.

'What Hinton said was this, sir. He took a squint towards the summerhouse after packing up his gear, and he saw a man dodge out and disappear into the trees. Then he heard an engine start in the lane and a car came by him, going towards Clyffe, just as he came out on the road. He says the man saw him and averted his face, but that he would know the man again.'

'Could he describe him?'

'Not very well, sir. Said he looked tallish, might be about fifty.'

'What about the car?'

'The same. All he could tell us was that it was a light colour.'

'Did you search the lane?'

'Well—no, sir. Though I've talked to one or two people who might have seen the car. But we reckoned that Hinton had made it all up, and that what he told us first was probably the truth.'

Tallish, and about fifty: not a riveting description, but such as it was it fitted Cleeve. And wasn't the poacher's story just too circumstantial to be dismissed as a desperate fiction? It should have stopped at the man vanishing into the trees, that would have answered Hinton's purpose, and while he might have added the car and the averted face, didn't the starting of the engine have a ring of conviction? Add it together, Cleeve parking in the lane, Pewsey parking where he could watch for Cleeve to arrive . . . clearly Pewsey hadn't gone there to shoot squirrels, and they weren't his reason for packing a gun.

Yet did it really hang together: wasn't he grasping at straws, trying to make sense of that fatal dab? After living with the problem for three days, the locals had no doubt what their attitude should be. For a time, they must have thought they had a chummie in Hinton, and a case against him was there for the making; but then they had cooled off, felt they'd pressured him into lies which, ironically, had given them the truth. Just a little old country job, so why was the Yard poking its nose in?

Well: time to tell them!

Gently opened his briefcase and laid the two photographs of Cleeve on the desk.

'Tallish, and now about fifty. This was the man who left the dab.'

They crowded to the desk to stare at these pictures of the man with the scared eyes, silent and expressionless, as though suspecting Gently of some deception. Pypard turned one over, but the verso was blank, just showed a faint browning of age. Finally Pypard dropped back on his chair, to stare a little sideways at Gently.

'Are you saying this is the man that Hinton saw, sir?'

Gently was relighting his pipe. 'Perhaps.'

'Does he have some connection with the Judge?'

After a puff or two, Gently nodded.

'Do we get to know his name, sir?'

'It wouldn't help you. The one he's using now will certainly be different.'

'But . . . does he have a record?'

'He has a record. Though nothing we know about for the past eighteen years.'

He took more puffs. Coming along the M4, he had made up the tale he was going to tell them—a tale that left a few loose ends, but which would give the locals all they needed to know. Whether they believed it was another matter. Pypard, for one, was nobody's fool.

'Now listen. Officially the man whose dab you sent us is listed as dead, and it was only by an outside chance that we were able to make the match. Eighteen years ago he escaped from custody after a conviction before Judge Pewsey, we know he got abroad and our information was that he died in a road accident. The conviction was for murder in the commission of a felony, at that time a capital offence, his appeal was turned down and he was waiting to be hung when he made a break from a prison hospital. His conviction had been unexpected. The prosecution had relied largely on a single witness. The conviction was almost certainly obtained by a harsh summing up by Judge Pewsey. So this man would have a grudge against Pewsey that might have led to his seeking revenge. And you find his dab on the door of a summerhouse inside which Pewsey lies shot. So we want that man and, in view of his past history, we want him sought with the minimum of publicity. That he's still alive and may have killed again is a feather in nobody's cap.'

They gazed at him silently during this recital, Canning's pale eyes, Pypard's dark. At the end of it he struck another match, and this too they watched in silence. Then Pypard said in a small voice:

'I don't remember that one, sir. Not a condemned man dodging the drop.'

'It happened eighteen years ago. He was thought to have died anyway. It was kept at low key.'

'That couldn't have been easy, sir. A job like that.'

'Take it the information is substantially correct.'

'Substantially, sir. Yes.'

'And if there are some other angles, none of them concern us here and now.'

Pypard's gaze held a moment, then he dropped his eyes. Canning apparently was staring at nothing. Gently puffed on. So they weren't going to buy it! And perhaps they would have been a pair of dumb cops if they had. If the thing had happened the way Gently had told it, wouldn't the story have been notorious to that very day?

'Anyway, now you know the situation. We want this man and we want him without fuss. We will have these photographs copied and circulated and the hotels and guest-houses in the area checked. The man's present age is forty-seven and he may have been at some pains to change his appearance. Also we have to assume that he's been living abroad, which may have left traces in his accent. One thing he won't know, that we are on to him and that his dabs are still on record. So he may be careless. With any luck, there will be more information along soon.'

Another silence! Then Pypard:

'Have we a reason to think he's still around here, sir?'

'Just this. He thinks he is safe, and may see no reason to leave the area.'

'He may have cleared off abroad again by now, sir.'

'In that case he'll be someone else's responsibility. But the trail begins here and here we shall try to pick it up.'

Pypard looked stubborn. 'It'll take manpower, sir.'

'So.'

'Well, it's all on a single dab, sir. This man coming back from the dead and all . . .'

He was interrupted by the phone, and grabbed it up.

'Yes, speaking . . . if I could have your name, sir . . .' Pypard's eyes grew steadily rounder. They could hear a steady, grumbling voice running on without a break. 'Just a minute, sir—I'll need your name! Oh Christ, the cheeky bastard . . .'

He leaned across the desk to jab a button. 'Gifford—see if you can trace that call!'

Seemingly Gifford couldn't. Pypard replaced the phone, a flush on his sallow face.

'Listen—I've just talked to a chummie who's telling me that the Judge bumped himself off—and he's telling me how! He did it with a walking stick, using it to press the trigger.'

Gently said: 'Was there a walking stick in the summerhouse?'

'Yes, sir!' Canning exclaimed. 'There was.'

'Lying near the body?'

'No, sir. It was standing by the wall, near the door.'

'Then someone must have been there to see it.'

Pypard was still glaring at the phone. 'I'll tell you something else, sir. Chummie had an accent. I don't know what, but he had one.'

'An obvious accent?'

Pypard shook his head. 'About what you were saying, as though he might have lived abroad. Oh glory be, do you think it was him, sir?'

Gently sucked on a pipe that had gone out again.

3

'That call was made from a box.'

It was ten minutes later, and in the interval packets of fish-and-chips and cans of beer had arrived, Canning had swiped a chair from reception, and now the three of them sat around, tucking in. But Pypard's mind wasn't on his job; he was cramming chips into his mouth almost resentfully. In the midst of his doubting, like a sign from above, the call had come, shattering disbelief; he couldn't get over it. He champed mechanically, his eyes distant and indignant.

The odour of fried fish swamped the small, untidy room, the window of which seemed never to have been opened. Yet outside, under shimmering midday sun, people were passing by in shirt-sleeves.

'It sounded like the chummie was next door. I'd swear that the call came from somewhere close. An educated sort of voice I'd say, not your average man-in-the-street.'

'Do you think what he said was possible, sir?' Canning asked.

Gently shrugged: 'Not if the stick put itself back by the door! Did the chauffeur mention it?'

'Said he touched nothing, sir. He just took one look, then went outside and was sick.'

'Was the stick fingerprinted?'

'No, sir. There seemed no occasion for it.'

'There weren't any games with sticks,' Pypard said bitterly. 'That was just chummie trying it on. That will be his tale when we pick him up, that he was watching through the window and saw it happen. But he isn't going to get away with that one. I reckon you were right, sir, and the gun was wiped. So chummie was in there, and he had the door shut—let him try to spruce his way out of that.'

'And he wouldn't have wiped the gun for nothing,' Canning said.

'Too true. His little dabs must have been all over it.'

'I reckon we'll have him, sir,' Canning said. 'With motive on top, we'll have him cold.'

Gently swallowed beer. 'First, we have to catch him!'

Pypard bolted a chip. 'That call was local, sir. But if chummie just came here to knock off the Judge, why is he still hanging about three days later?'

'He's not your usual chummie.'

'All the same, sir.'

'He's waited eighteen years for this. He thinks he is fireproof, a man from nowhere. He might well have hung on to watch events.'

Pypard stared. 'And to take the juice, sir?'

'He might find it amusing to watch us react.'

Pypard drank. 'No,' he said. 'No, sir. My bet is that he lives around here. If he's fireproof, like you say, what was to stop him coming back and settling down? He's a dead man, we can't touch him. And there's been no hanging since 'sixty-five.'

'I still want a check of hotels and guest-houses.'

'Well sir, if you say so. But he could just as well be a tradesman in the High, or the man who calls the numbers at bingo.'

And so he could. For all they knew, Cleeve might have returned several years ago, be now a familiar figure somewhere: a man of substance, even. But in that case, wouldn't he have kept his head down and shunned the risk of taking such a revenge? Much more likely that he came as a stranger, and able to vanish again into his nowhere. Gently balled his fish-and-chip paper and polished his fingers.

'Get these photographs copied and circulating. Now I'm going to borrow your Inspector to show me round Erchildown New Place.'

'Do you want me to give the lady a ring, sir?'

Gently paused, then shook his head.

Outside, after the fug in Pypard's office, the fresh air tasted like wine.

The smooth green swell of the downs grew closer as they drove down the Prior's Compton road, and one of the strange White Horses of the district began to show on their grassy flanks. A curious animal, it more resembled a heraldic leopard than a horse, an abstract symbolism that dated back perhaps to Celtic ritual.

On either hand verges were clothed with cow parsley and hawthorn hedges stooped in blossom; field-oaks were powdered with amber leaf, and in a pasture, horse-chestnuts held candles to the sun.

Then, ahead of them, rose a spur of the downs, entirely chequered with the young greens of trees, below which nestled roofs and the spire and squat tower of a church.

'Erchildown, sir.'

'Are those Pewsey's woods?'

'Yes sir. All his.'

The village was centred upon a green across which the church and a pub, the Cross Keys, faced each other. Followed half a mile in which they skirted the woods, oaks, beeches, and ashes knobbed with dark flower; then they arrived at a pair of iron gates through which could be seen the front of a small country house. Gently turned in. A drive led through rhododendrons and crossed a stone bridge to a sweep before the house. There was parked a glinting black Mercedes, and Gently dropped his Rover in beside it.

'Pewsey's car?'

'Yes, sir. But not the one he was driving on Friday.'

Gently stared about him. Silent, complete, the Judge's house stood below its hanging woods. Though small it was architecturally exquisite, a page from some Regency artist's sketchbook. Steps rose to a cupolaed portico, sash windows mounted in exact progression, at each end of the roof-cornice reared a slender pinnacle and delicate quoining framed the flush stonework. Below the sweep lawns descended to a small lake, the work of Repton or a disciple, and a screen of trees hid the road except for the glimpse one caught at the gates. Exquisite: yet somehow chilling, even on a warm day in May, when birdsong sounded far and near and the fragrance of new leaf was everywhere. An exercise in aesthetics rather than a house for someone to live in. And shut away from the common world: to this had a hanging judge retired.

'Here's the lady, sir,' Canning murmured.

A woman had appeared at the top of the steps. She stood in the portico, staring down at them, a challenging figure clad in black.

'That is Mrs Pewsey . . . ?'

'Yes, sir. She's the second Mrs Pewsey.'

The Judge had been seventy-eight, the woman on the steps was scarcely fifty.

She came down to them.

'You have brought some fresh news for me, Inspector?'

'Actually . . . no, ma'am!' Canning stammered. 'I'm just here with the Chief Superintendent.'

'Oh—a Chief Superintendent now, is it?' She inspected Gently with cool eyes. 'But isn't this doing too much honour to the arrest of a simple poacher?'

'We haven't come about that, ma'am,' Canning gulped.

'Really? Then why have you come?'

'Well . . . just routine really, ma'am. The Chief Superintendent wants to see things for himself.'

She was fifty or a shade over, but still a piquant, attractive woman. Her nose was slightly snub and she had a shapely but determined mouth. Her smooth, rounded cheeks had a pallor that was perhaps being emphasized by her dress; her figure was firm, and her step had been elastic as she came down the steps. The Judge's widow. If she had grief, it was certainly not for public display.

'Just a few questions, Mrs Pewsey. If it isn't putting you out.'

'Thank you, Superintendent, I am familiar with the ways of the law.'

'Then perhaps, if we could go inside?'

Her stare said she would like to refuse, but after a moment she motioned with her head and turned to lead them up the steps. They entered a lofty hall that featured a sweeping, cast-iron staircase, then passed through into a drawing-room with windows looking down to the lake. Mrs Pewsey indicated chairs. She herself took a seat by a window. The room was furnished in modern style, with tapestry-covered chairs, and smelled of polish and dead flowers.

'So what can I tell you, Superintendent?'

'First, if your husband ever received threatening letters.'

'My, my!' She had been gazing through the window, but now turned her head sharply. 'Has something fresh turned up then?'

'If you would kindly answer the question.'

'Very well. The answer is yes, Arthur received them all the time. He was a public figure, and a judge. It is one of the commonplaces of the profession. Whenever there was an important criminal case being tried they came as regularly as the morning papers.'

'Would he have had one lately?'

'For all I know. But if he did, he didn't tell me. Sometimes he handed them to the police, but mostly just destroyed them.'

'Perhaps he received an anonymous phone call?'

'Again, not to my knowledge.'

'Has he spoken lately of any of his cases?'

She shook her head, her eyes probing. 'But you must have some reason for asking this.'

Gently met her stare blank-faced. 'We have evidence that another person was present at the summerhouse.'

'You mean Hinton?'

'Not Hinton.'

'How reliable is it—this evidence?'

'Quite reliable. Evidence of the presence of a person who might have wished your husband harm.'

She continued to stare, though not quite at Gently. Her face was as empty as his own: a face naturally inexpressive, as though trained long since to hide its emotions.

'And you know the name of this man?'

'We know that person's identity.'

'And have you arrested—that person?'

'We are pursuing our enquiries.'

'Then you haven't arrested him. And in some way, he is connected with one of Arthur's cases. I suppose you haven't come to warn me that I should be on my guard too?'

'I doubt if you are in any danger, Mrs Pewsey.'

'That's a comfort. Am I to be told the man's name?'

'You will be told when our enquiries are completed.'

'If I knew who he was, I might perhaps be able to help you.'

She turned her face to the window again, a touch of pique in the action. Though her expression was so well controlled, nervous tension appeared in a furtive clasping of her hands. An interesting woman: and nearly thirty years younger than the hawk-faced man she had married. Her dress, though sombre, couldn't quite conceal the vibrant figure beneath it.

'Are you expecting a visitor, Mrs Pewsey?'

'What? No!' She turned about instantly.

'Then perhaps you can spare the time to help me in another matter.'

'Of course. Ask me what you like. As I told you, I am familiar with the law. My first husband was a QC, so I have been in the profession all my life.'

'In that case you will appreciate the importance we attach to checking and re-checking people's movements. I would like you to go over the events of Friday, beginning with Friday morning.'

'Well—if I must.' She gave her hands a hitch. 'As you may have been told, we were entertaining guests the evening before.'

'Your husband behaved quite normally then.'

'Oh quite.' Her eyes were large for an instant. 'I merely mentioned it because our guests didn't leave until one-thirty, and as a result neither Arthur nor I rose very early on Friday morning. I had breakfast in bed at about nine-thirty, and I assume that Arthur had his in bed too.'

'You slept in separate rooms?'

'Certainly. Ours was a marriage of companionship. Arthur was a friend of the Levesons, my first husband's family, and I'd known him all my married life. He had two married daughters, one older than myself, and I had a son going through law school. It seemed appropriate to join forces. Arthur was quite active, in spite of his age.'

'A successful arrangement.'

'Entirely successful.' She dwelt briefly on the words. 'And so, on Friday, I didn't see Arthur much before we went in to lunch.'

'You knew of his plans for the afternoon.'

'I knew about the LMA meeting, naturally. He asked me if he could use my car, since Dennis, that's our chauffeur, had to go into town shopping.'

'What was his behaviour at lunch?'

'Perfectly normal, I would have said.'

'Did his dress surprise you?'

'His dress?'

'He was scarcely dressed for a formal occasion.'

She checked. 'I suppose I might have been surprised, but in some things Arthur was an eccentric. Plus-four suits were his favourites, and LMA meetings are not so very formal.'

'It didn't occur to you that he might have changed his plans.'

She shook her head. 'No.'

'Looking back, you can remember nothing said that might have suggested it.'

She went on shaking her head. 'At lunch, there wasn't much conversation. We were probably both feeling fagged after the late night. Dennis came in to get some money and to ask what meat we would like for the weekend, and Arthur chose a leg of pork. I don't remember anything else.'

'The chauffeur left when?'

'While we were still at lunch. He took Sarah, our maid, into town with him. Then, at two, Arthur went for the car, and I saw him drive off past the house.'

'The last time you saw him.'

'Yes.'

'Didn't it strike you as odd that he should have left so early?'

Her mouth was tight for a moment. 'What he actually said was that he intended to call at his tailor's first. I knew he had a suit on order, so I never gave it a second thought.'

Her tone was sour, and she'd looked away from Gently, her clasped hands twisting. And suddenly the black dress seemed a farce, a sham gesture to the proprieties. Gently said:

'Did you love your husband?'

'I regard that as an impertinence.'

'He was an old man.'

'He was my husband.'

'But an old man.'

She turned her face to the window.

'So your husband left at two, and the chauffeur and the maid had left earlier. Then the only people in the house would have been yourself and your housekeeper.'

'If you know that, why ask?'

She was defiantly facing him again. Yet something had changed, if it were only an extra hostility in her voice.

'You are the person who can best tell me.'

'I have already given that information. Yes, there was just Rose and myself. Till Dennis came back at half-past four.'

'That was usual on a Friday.'

'And if it was?'

'Please continue your account.'

She eyed him malignantly. 'Rose was in the kitchen, I went to my room to lie down. Arthur might have been an old man, but he could stand late nights better than I could.'

'You spent the time sleeping?'

The hands moved. 'I was probably asleep some of the time. Then I read and listened to the radio. I rang down for Rose to fetch me a pot of tea.'

'When was that?'

'Oh—about three.'

'So you may have been awake at two-forty.'

'I may or I may not. In any case I didn't hear the shot.'

'Your housekeeper heard it.'

'Rose was in the kitchen, and that is at the back of the house. My bedroom is at the front, where I probably couldn't have heard it anyway. The summerhouse is through the woods.'

'How long would it take to walk there from here?'

'How should I know?'

'Twenty minutes?'

Her stare was ferocious.

'When did you come down from your room?'

'I heard Dennis return and went down to see he'd brought everything I wanted. On Fridays we have a high tea at six and I expected Arthur back before then. When he failed to arrive I rang the LMA secretary, who told me that Arthur hadn't been to the meeting, then I asked Rose if Arthur had said anything to her, and she remembered hearing a shot in the woods.'

'Which was quite a usual thing.'

'Entirely usual. So I supposed that Arthur had changed his mind about the meeting. I sent Dennis up to tell him the meal was ready, and Dennis found his body in the summerhouse.'

'And then?'

'Then I rang the police, of course.'

'You didn't first check on what the chauffeur told you?'

'No. Why should I?'

'Your husband might still have been alive, even though unconscious and severely wounded.'

The hands clenched tight. 'It seemed unlikely! If he had been lying there three hours with a hole in his chest. Anyway, Dennis had no doubts, and I didn't feel I could face going up there myself.'

'You didn't ring a doctor.'

'It seemed pointless. Rose gave me a brandy, and then I rang the police.'

'You showed great presence of mind, Mrs Pewsey.'

'And that, I take it, is not a crime.'

The tension was explosive: Canning sat by scarcely daring to take breath, and for some moments the only sounds were those of birds, through an open window. One heard the alarm toll of a blackbird, the plaintive notes of chaffinch and warbler; and, from high in the woods, the echoing laugh of a woodpecker.

And the woman had turned to the window again. From outside one would see her erect, black-clad figure. In a room that, despite the vernal greens all about, smelled only of dead flowers.

'Thank you, Mrs Pewsey.'

'Oh please don't mention it.'

'If I may, I would like a word with your staff.'

'I'm sure you would. And if I know my staff, you will find them still hanging about in the kitchen.'

Gently rose. Mrs Pewsey didn't budge. Followed by Canning, Gently left the room.

The kitchen was a long, high room in which some modern appliances looked alien and defensive: there was still a great stone sink, perhaps intended for scouring carcasses, and shelf upon shelf of copper utensils.

In the centre stood a stout trestle table, and about this the staff were seated at a meal. Conversation ceased when the policemen entered and four faces turned towards them resentfully.

'Don't get up! I just want a few words.'

It was the housekeeper principally whom Gently put through her paces. A plumpish woman with a fresh, plump face, she answered his questions in a rolling country accent. The maid and the chauffeur confirmed their stories, the gardener hadn't been there at all. But the housekeeper had actually heard the shot, a distinction that she was happy to dwell on.

'It was at twenty to three, that I'll swear, because I was timing a cake in the oven. That'll be his lordship banging away, I said to myself, never giving it another thought.'

'How soon afterwards did Mrs Pewsey ring?'

'I can't tell you exactly, m'dear. Truth, I thought she had gone off out, but she says it was only to the stables.'

'You saw her go out?'

'I saw her cross the yard. She must have come back while I was in the cellar.'

The chauffeur had seen no walking stick; he had almost fallen over his feet to get out of the summerhouse.

They passed out into a wide, paved yard on the far side of which ranged the stables. There a grey mare in one of several loose-boxes advanced her head to eye the two men benevolently.

'And now for that summerhouse . . . !'

'This way, sir.'

Canning ushered Gently to a gate in the yard. Beyond it lay walled kitchen gardens, and then a gate giving access to the woods. Here a winding path rose steeply beneath the deep shade of beeches, soon losing sight of the house except for an occasional glimpse of the roofs.

'So what do we make of that, sir?' Canning asked as they laboured up the path. 'The lady didn't like what you were getting at. I thought she would blow her top.'

'Just establishing facts,' Gently grunted.

'She could have been up here,' Canning said. 'And then dodged back, and rung the housekeeper to make like she had never left her room. It's on the cards, sir. And then we'd have a right old job on our hands.'

'So let's not rush our fences.'

'Then if there's a boyfriend on top, sir—and if he was the bloke who left the dab.'

'Just now we'll stick to the facts we've got.'

They went on climbing through beeches, oaks and occasional groups of chestnut, trees probably coeval with the house and planted by the man who devised the lake. The wood was dense. In no direction could one see gaps in the green gloom, and except under the beeches the woodland floor was overgrown with bracken, honeysuckle and snowberry. They disturbed a jay, noisy and clumsy, and caught the yellow flash of the rump of the woodpecker. Then wicked eyes stared at them from around boles, followed quickly by grey puffs floating away through the branches.

'Plenty to shoot at, sir,' Canning breathed. 'Plenty across where we left the car, too.'

'Then why only two cartridges?'

'Could have forgotten them, sir.'

'Cartridges are the first thing a shooting man checks.'

But now the woods were levelling off and the shatter of sunlight showed ahead. They came out on the brow of the ridge with a brilliantly-lit prospect ranged before them. Much closer now was the White Horse and the sheep-bitten turf of the downs, and one could see clearly marked a pattern of mounds and ancient earthworks. The ridge descended in a bracken slope to an area of blackthorn scrub and gorse, and to the left was broken into by what may have been an old extraction of gravel. There trees came down to a cliffy edge and there lay overgrown ruins. Further on was the minor road, white-edged with hawthorn, departing into distant trees.

'This is it, sir.'

A hundred yards higher up stood a green-painted, octagonal summerhouse, at the edge of the trees, facing the prospect, and partly overgrown by tangling honeysuckle.

'A queer old place, sir . . .'

The odds were that it was at least a century old. It had a lofted roof, almost a spire, surmounted by a glazed lantern. The wall panels were planked diagonally and decorated with split timber, and little leaded-paned window bays were supported by crooked sections of barked boughs.

Though old it was immensely solid, and the notion of using it as a prison by no means far-fetched.

'Let's take a look.'

Canning produced a key and unlocked the heavily-framed door. The first thing one saw was the chalked outline which the locals had drawn on the planked floor. Of blood there was little, mostly scatter-drops, some of them flung on the varnished walls. The summerhouse was unfurnished but a number of cushions lay in a pile on a fitted bench.

'The stick, sir—it's still here.'

It stood in the angle of the door post, and moreover in a

situation where it couldn't have been seen from outside. But it was a natural ash-plant, with a rind unapt for dabs. Gently brushed it with a finger and the finger came away laden with dust.

'That wasn't the way of it . . .'

So what was the way—what had happened in that dim little place, where, when the door was shut, you were enclosed in a sort of grubby twilight? Had Cleeve contrived to lure Pewsey in there, then to find himself on the end of a gun? What was the end of the plot to have been, if not Pewsey's body sprawled on the floor? Blackmail was out. Cleeve had no hold on the man who had sent him to the gallows.

'Show me the warren.'

'Over there, sir.'

Canning pointed to the pit excavated in the ridge. From the summerhouse it was three hundred yards, with the edge of the pit concealed by gorse. They tramped across to it. Below were sandy hummocks, tufted with bracken, and at least a score of white scuts bobbed away as they peered down. The floor of the pit ran out into gorse and blackthorn at no great distance from the minor road; from below was an easy ascent up the shallowly-sloping side.

'From there, Hinton says he saw a man leave the summer-house.'

'Yes, sir. That's his tale.'

Gently clambered down. It was possible, but at the distance Hinton wouldn't have seen him very clearly.

'And the lane—where's that?'

'Hold hard, sir!'

Suddenly Canning dropped flat; he put out a restraining hand as Gently climbed back to the level.

'What is it?'

'A chummie, sir—he's just sneaked out of the ruins.'

'A chummie?'

'A tallish bloke, fawn jacket, tan trousers.'

'Going where?'

'Towards the summerhouse—no, he's stopped—he's seen

the door open. Oh blast!' Canning leaped up. 'Come on, sir—we can have him!'

Canning sprinted in the direction of the ruins, leaving Gently to trail in his rear. Just as the local man vanished amongst the old stonework, an engine started some way off. Gently plunged into the ruins, which were overgrown with brambles and saplings, hearing Canning bawling ahead and the sound of the car accelerating in low gear. He burst out into a lane in time to see Canning disappear round a bend; but the sound of the car was already distant, speeding along the minor road. He caught up with Canning.

'The bastard, sir! It was Hinton's chummie all over again.'

'Did you get his number?'

'Sorry sir, but he was round the corner and away. But the colour of the car was a light beige, and he was tallish—a hundred to one it was the same chummie.'

'And each time driving off in the same direction.'

Canning's eyes glistened. 'The Clyffe way, sir. He might turn off at one of the side roads, but if we could just get to a blower . . .'

Gently shrugged: without the car-number, what would be the point? And by the time they got down to the phone at the house, the man would probably have gone to ground anyway.

'This time we've lost him, but there may be others. We'll ask Clyffe to keep an eye open.'

'I'm sorry, sir. It's my fault.'

'At least we know now that Hinton wasn't romancing.'

They relocked the summerhouse and left it to brood in its gloom. When they emerged again in the yard behind the house, the housekeeper hastened out to them.

'Your lot has been on the phone, m'dears, says as how you're to ring them back.'

'Where is Mrs Pewsey?'

'That's another thing. She's gone up to lie down and doesn't want to be disturbed.'

Canning went in to make the call, Gently strolled round to sit in his car. As he waited, he thought he saw a curtain twitch in an upper window. Otherwise all was still about the Judge's exquisite house, its pinnacles, its trees, its lake on which waterfowl were floating.

Canning came out.

'Here's a turn-up, sir!'

He got in the car beside Gently.

'One of my lads has just picked up Hinton as he was boarding the London coach. He was wearing his best duds, and had better than two hundred quid in his pocket.'

4

'If you find a case that the Public Prosecutor will look at, it would be a lucky break for everyone.'

The Assistant Commissioner's words passed through Gently's mind as he studied Hinton across Pypard's desk.

If a scapegoat was needed, Hinton was he: a man who struck you at once as a probable delinquent, a furtive, bovine-faced fellow with a drooping lower lip that revealed long yellow teeth. There was something unhealthily sensual about him, his baggy red cheeks and shapeless body: was he mentally retarded? At least you sensed a barrier between his mind and any common intelligence.

Dressed in a black serge suit, white shirt and red tie, he stood breathing through his mouth and gazing vacantly. Besides convictions for poaching and being drunk and disorderly he had one for carnal relations with a minor.

'So where did you get this money, Hinton?'

For the interrogation, Canning had stationed himself beside Gently. Pypard was sitting at the end of the desk, his shrewd eyes watching everything.

'Now you've made me miss my bus, haven't you?'

'Never mind the bus! What about the money?'

'But that's the only bus out of Mazey. I tell you . . .'

'Where did you get two hundred quid?'

It was as though Canning's questions were punching air. No wonder they'd had doubts about Hinton's testimony! Simply to connect with his mind was a feat, let alone to squeeze valid information from it. In his slurred, grumbling voice he seemed to be responding from a different world.

'Listen. This is your money, isn't it?'

'I've got some money . . . why shouldn't I have?'

'So where did you get it?'

'What? Farmer Woolley paid me. That is . . .'

'Woolley paid you two hundred pounds?'

'I've been saving up, haven't I?'

'You saved it from your wages?'

'What? Why shouldn't I?'

'You with a family of six kids?'

Hinton's small eyes kept staring stupidly at the desk, where the contents of his pockets were spread out. They included a pipe, a pouch and a horn-handled clasp knife, as well as the wad of notes, mostly ones and fivers.

'Who gave you that money, Hinton?'

'Haven't I said? . . . old Woolley . . .'

'I think you pinched it.'

'What? Who off?'

'That's what I'm asking you.'

'Arr. But I never pinched it.'

'You pinched it to slide off to London with. Mazey's getting too hot for you, Hinton. You decided it was time to sling your hook.'

'What me? Why should I do that.'

'Because we're on to you Hinton, that's why. You were mixed up with the shooting job, you know that, and so do we.'

'Arr, I tell you. I hears the shot.'

'So what about the rest you haven't told us.'

'I tell you about the man—'

'Never mind about the man!'

'Well there you are, m'dear. I sees him, though.'

Was he really as thick as he seemed, or was it a strain of animal cunning? After each response his mouth hung open, and needed to be jacked up afresh for the next. Yet he was turning Canning's attack neatly, the Inspector was making no ground at all. And Pypard was drinking it in with sly amusement: now Gently would learn something, his expression seemed to say.

'So perhaps you'll tell us this, Hinton. Just why were you dodging off to London?'

'Arr, I've missed my bus, I have. Your bloke come in there and haul me off it.'

'Answer the question!'

'I don't reckon it's right, I don't. Not in front of all them people. 'Cause why shouldn't I go to London? I've got a right as well as they have.'

'Not when we've told you to stay here you haven't!'

'And that money's my own, arr.'

'Look Hinton, playing dumb will get you nowhere.'

'I saved it up, you ask the missus.'

Gently said: 'I come from London. Where were you going to stay, Mr Hinton?'

For the first time Hinton's eyes lifted, appeared to creep into a sort of focus. They met Gently's just for an instant, then wandered off and sank again to the desk.

'Little place I know.'

'Near the coach station?'

'Arr.'

'How long did you mean to stay there?'

'Don't know, do I. A day or two.'

'Just till things had quietened down.'

'Arr, maybe. I don't know.'

'What tobacco do you smoke?'

'Condor, don't I.'

'Would you like to smoke now?'

'These buggers won't let me.'

'They'll let you.'

His eyes lifted again, to squint first at the poker-faced Pypard, then the wrathful Canning. Then he took a plug of tobacco from the pouch and began to shave slices with the clasp knife. It was an unhurried process, completely absorbing him, as though his mind had room for only one thing at a time. So far he had displayed no nervousness: you wondered if he was capable of feeling it.

At last he lit the pipe with care and adjusted the ash with his thumb.

'You smoke a pipe, zir?'

'I smoke a pipe.'

'Arr. Beats all your rotten fags.'

Now he wasn't exactly looking at Gently, but his eyes rested somewhere below Gently's chin.

'How many ferrets have you?'

Though he had his pipe, Hinton's mouth still tended to sag. He puffed at it rapidly, as though tasting something strange, but always his teeth came into view again.

'Six, zir. Real goers. See 'em set about the rats.'

'And the rabbits?'

'You can lose the buggers. Won't come out, often.'

'What about Friday?'

'There you are, then.' He exhibited a finger with a crooked gash. 'Reckon I give her a squeeze, like, when I heard that gun go off.'

'You weren't expecting it.'

'Not me, m'dear.'

'You had seen and heard nothing before the shot?'

'Ask yourself, zir. I wouldn't have been there if I'd seen folk up around.'

'What about on the road?'

'Arr, there's that.' Hinton tasted his pipe a few times. 'That'll be half a mile from my house, but I kept away from the road, see. I got my sack and my little old dog, I come away along the hedge. Might have been a car pass. Come to think of it, I believe I heard one.'

'A car you saw?'

'Didn't see it, did I?'

'Which way was it heading?'

'Upalong.'

'Could it have been the one you say was parked in the lane?'

'I reckon. Aren't so many cars go by there.'

'So why didn't you tell us before!' Canning broke in. 'You never mentioned a car passing you.'

'Only just remembered it, m'dear.'

'And now what else are you going to remember!'

Hinton's small eyes flickered briefly towards Canning, then settled again below Gently's chin. About him was something primitive and monumental, like the downs themselves and their dimpling earthworks.

'Could you see the lane?'

'Reckon.'

'What about the gap where the Judge's car was found?'

'Up round in the trees, it was. Couldn't see that from down below.'

'And you couldn't see the car parked in the lane.'

'I'm telling you, m'dear. He'd shoved it up by the old house, where I hear him start it later on.'

'So you arrived at the warren. Tell me what happened.'

Was that pushing him a bit too hard? His lip drooped even lower and his rabbity teeth mauled the pipe-stem.

'Got my nets staked out, didn't I? And the little old dog sits watching . . . nigh on speak to you, she will. Nothing gets by her, I tell you.'

'You heard nothing at all.'

'Not down there. Nor the little old dog didn't, neither. She'd have told me. But not a whimper. Just sits perked, waiting for the rabbits.'

'And then?'

'I've got Zoe in my hand, ready to shove her into the burrow . . . then that old bugger lets go with his gun, and she nearly have a lump out of my finger. Swear, you bet I swear. He should have been safe down in Mazey. I stuff Zoe back in her bag and get my nets up in a hurry.'

'Why didn't you clear out straight away?'

'What? With that old bugger around? I sit tight for a minute, I tell you, and the little old dog she sit tight too. Then I didn't hear no more, so I draws up the bank for a squint round.'

'Tell me exactly what you saw.'

'Arr. Well first off I didn't see nothing. Then this bloke comes flying out of the summerhouse and runs off into the trees.'

'Into the trees?'

'That's what I'm saying. He didn't hang about, I can tell you.'

'The trees behind the summerhouse?'

'Why yes.'

'Not in the direction of the car in the lane?'

Hinton chewed on his pipe, the focus beginning to drain from his eyes.

'You've got him, sir,' Canning muttered. 'This doesn't square with what he told us before.'

'How long after that when you heard the car start?'

Hinton's lip rose and drooped a couple of times. 'I reckon . . . maybe he dodged out again. I didn't hang about to see.'

'Yes, twice likely,' Canning sneered.

'Reckon he could. If he was quick.'

'So now we've got two of them,' Canning sneered. 'One running into the wood, one starting the car. Sure there weren't any more?'

Hinton's eyes were vacant. 'It was the same bloke . . . the same one in the car.'

'You recognised him,' Gently said. 'The same man each time.'

'Yes . . . I reckon . . .'

'Can you describe him?'

Oddly, you felt it was some discrepancy in Hinton's recollections that was confusing him, and that it was genuine: he was honestly thrown by something that didn't quite add up.

'Taller than me, he was. And he didn't move like a youngster.'

'What was he wearing?'

'Couldn't say . . . good clothes, I'd reckon.'

'Light or dark?'

'Arr, now. On the light side, I'd say.'

'How long after the shot when you first saw him?'

'Be a minute or two, wouldn't it . . . maybe five, maybe ten. I kept my head down for a bit.'

'And from then till when the engine started?'

Clearly the timing was what was worrying him. After some jerky drags on his pipe, he said:

'So I don't know how . . . only he got there.'

'Because it was the same man driving the car?'

'Well yes. It was him all right.'

'Though you had seen him only briefly up at the summer-house, you could be sure he was the same?'

'Well . . . I reckon. He passed right close. He saw me and I saw him. He turned his head, but I saw him plain, man about my age, going grey.'

'A man you would recognise again.'

'It wasn't a face you'd forget, was it.'

'Now I'm going to show you some photographs of a man that were taken eighteen years ago.'

Pypard produced the Cleeve photographs and handed them to Hinton. He stared from one to the other stupidly, as though at some problem hopeless of solution.

'He's older, is he?'

'Eighteen years older.'

'Reckon it'd make a bit of difference.'

'Could he be your man?'

'Reckon . . . maybe.'

But clearly the photographs struck no chord.

Canning said: 'Now let's have the truth, Hinton. A man in a car was all you saw. The rest you just dreamed up to try to get us off your back.'

Hinton's lip drooped. 'I see him up there . . .'

'I'll tell you who you saw!' Canning snarled. 'You saw Judge Pewsey looking down at you, just as you were putting in a ferret. That's when you squeezed it and got your finger bitten—when you found yourself staring into his gun. He was laying for you, Hinton. He wasn't a fool. He knew you were getting the down through his maid.'

'But I never set eyes on him—'

'Oh yes you did. And he marched you off at the point of his gun. And it was the third time, wasn't it, Hinton—you were due for the chop, and you knew it.'

'But it's like I said!'

'Tell that to the jury, we're not believing it any longer. You did for yourself, Hinton, the moment you stepped on the London coach.'

It was the case the A.C. was yearning for, and just for a moment it seemed it might stick. Hinton was gaping helplessly, eyes stricken, mouth a-quiver. He was staring into the gulf Canning had opened and beginning to realise it might yawn for him, that assertions of innocence were no longer good enough. Yet they were all he had to offer.

He pulled his mouth together. 'Listen! . . .'

But the moment was shattered by a tap on the door. A young D.C. entered, his face full of hot intelligence.

'What do you want, Holt?' Canning rapped.

'Sir, I've just come from the Red Lion. They think a man like the one we're looking for may have spent Thursday night there.'

'Thursday night?'

'Yes, sir. And they say the man had a slight accent.'

Hinton jerked suddenly out of his trance. 'The Red Lion—that's where I seen him!' He gazed at Gently. 'I knew it, zir, I knew I'd seen that bugger before.'

Canning glared at Hinton. 'Which bugger?'

'Why, him as passed me at the warren. Seen him putting down pints, I have, a couple of times, maybe three.'

Canning looked as though he might have hit him.

'You stupid bloody liar,' he said.

The interior of the Red Lion matched the exterior in elaborate ornateness; one entered an ambience of panelled walls, moulded drop-ceilings and glowing mahogany. Behind a reception-desk that resembled the counter of an old-fashioned bank the manager awaited them, a small-featured man with slicked hair.

'I'm Heywood . . . this fellow isn't wanted for anything serious, is he?'

'We wish to talk to him.'

'But I mean, it's nothing . . . I've got our reputation to think of.'

'Let's go through to your office.'

'Of course.'

Heywood darted an anxious look down the hall, to where, in a large lounge, customers were sitting at afternoon-tea. Some others stood chatting in the foyer and two waitresses were tripping back and forth, while, in an empty bar-room, one could see a man gesticulating to a phone.

They went through the flap into an office furnished with a roll-top desk and a massive safe. In a flutter, Heywood cleared two chairs on which open box-files had been left.

'We always try to help the police, but—'

'I would like to see your register.'

'This man was perfectly respectable, in fact the sort of guest we mainly cater for.'

In the register he had given his name as Hamilton, nationality British, address simply 'London', the entry written in a clear, educated hand with the letters neatly formed.

'Has his room been let since?'

'Yes. It was reoccupied the same evening . . . did you wish to see it?'

Gently shrugged: the chances of dabs there now were slight.

'Describe him to me, Mr Heywood.'

'Certainly.' Heywood cleared his throat. 'Well, he was dressed nicely in a grey mixture suit, one that didn't come off the peg, a quiet silk tie and tan shoes of excellent quality.'

'He impressed you as affluent.'

'Exactly. The sort of guest we're glad to see. His manner, too. I put him down as a professional man of some sort. I took his registration myself. He said he was touring in the West Country, would probably stay over the weekend, but might decide to move on. If he hadn't registered himself as British I might have taken him for a colonial, there was just that difference in his speech. But perhaps he came from Ulster or Scotland.'

'And he resembled the photographs.'

'Let me put it this way. When I was shown the photographs I at once thought of him. He was older, of course, and greying, but there was the same wave in his hair. I can't swear it was the same man, but certainly he bore a close resemblance.'

'Height and build?'

'About your height but his build was slimmer.'

'Colour of eyes?'

Heywood shook his head. 'Eye-colour is something one rarely notices.'

'Any other peculiarities?'

He thought about it, but shook his head again. 'All I can say is that he struck me as respectable and that I would have been willing to cash a cheque for him.'

The ultimate accolade of a hotel-keeper! And coming from a man who clearly knew his business. If this were Cleeve, then Cleeve had prospered, wherever his eighteen years had been spent. An ex-claims clerk . . . was he following his old trade in pastures new . . . as a 'Mr Hamilton'?

'What make of car was he driving?'

'Your man asked me that. I didn't see his car myself, and he was only here for twenty-four hours. Rudge, who brought up his luggage, says it was a medium fawn saloon, but he didn't notice the make. So it couldn't have been anything special.'

'At what time did he book in?'

'At four p.m.'

'Would you know how he spent the evening?'

'He was in for dinner, and later I saw him in the lounge with a map and a guidebook. Jane, who was on the desk, said he consulted the phone directory, but he didn't make a call.'

'And on the Friday?'

'He went out after breakfast. Rudge says it was at about ten. He left word at the desk that he would be out for lunch. He came in at three-thirty to cancel his booking.'

The timing was right.

'What excuse did he give?'

'Just that he had decided to move on.'

'Did he seem in a hurry?'

'Well . . . now you mention it. He didn't wait for Rudge to fetch his luggage.'

'Anything else you noticed?'

Heywood stared. 'He looked somehow untidy and his hands were grubby. He paid me with two twenty-pound notes and seemed to have plenty more in his wallet.'

'Do you have the notes?'

'They've been banked.'

'Of course, he didn't mention a destination?'

'Since he was only here for such a short time there would scarcely have been mail for us to send on.'

Had it been Cleeve? The details fitted, yet identification was still less than positive. Some innocent tourist having a passing resemblance might well have behaved in the same way. Still, it rested on that one dab whether Cleeve was involved, or even in existence . . .

Heywood was jiffling.

'I must insist again that this man's appearance was in no way suspicious. I don't know what he is supposed to have done, but I feel you are making a big mistake.'

'Tell me, have you ever seen him before—perhaps as a customer in the bar?'

'No . . . at least, not to my knowledge. I can't remember every casual customer.'

'On second thoughts, I will examine his room. And I would like to borrow your register.'

He brushed Heywood's objections aside. Canning fetched in his assistants and their equipment. Four of them, they marched up the stairs behind Heywood to a first-floor bedroom overlooking the High Street. Its occupant, an elderly lady, looked on bemused as the men went to work with insufflator and camera, and grimy smears began to spread over immaculate ivory paintwork. But it was effort almost certainly in vain. Three times since Friday the room had been cleaned, the basin and glass shelf wiped, a duster put over the rest. Dabs would be found, but they wouldn't be Cleeve's; and the register was probably a forlorn hope too.

'That's about it, sir.'

'We'll take the register with us.'

Heywood was looking daggers at the soiled paint. He went down with them as far as reception, then stood staring after them as they left.

'So where does that leave us, sir?'

An hour later they were drinking tea in Pypard's office: over-brewed tea in chipped mugs, which seemed in some way to epitomise the situation. Pypard had gone out, and in his absence Gently had ventured to prize open the window; but though now it admitted a moan of traffic, the atmosphere in the office remained much as before. Meanwhile the efforts of the dabs team had produced nothing: register and all, they had drawn a blank.

'I look at it this way, sir.'

For a while, Canning had sat brooding over his mug. Now he drank up with an air of decision and set the mug down.

'We don't know when chummie left his dab in the summer-house, but we do know when Hinton was there. And we can shoot holes through Hinton's story, show how he came up with different versions.'

Gently gulped tea. 'Yet when I arrived here you had decided to let Hinton drop!'

'Yes sir, but that was then.' Canning's pale eyes gazed earnestly at Gently. 'But now two things—Hinton has tried to make a run for it, and there's your point about the cartridges. The Judge didn't go there to shoot squirrels, he went on purpose to catch Hinton. And there's a way to prove it. I'll have a talk with the maid, find out if the Judge tried to pump her.'

'The Judge was there to catch someone. But it wasn't Hinton.'

'With respect, sir, he did have it in for Hinton. A couple of private prosecutions, and now a chance to fit him up proper.'

'But did he need a gun to do that?'

'I'd say it wasn't out of character, sir. And unless he arrested Hinton on the job he might have trouble making it stick.'

'Chummie was there. It supports Hinton's story.'

'But Hinton's story contradicts itself, sir. He says he saw chummie dive into the trees. But then the next moment he's driving off in a car. And none of this Hinton tells us straight off, it's a tale he's been building up since Friday. I reckon if I have another go at him, sir, I can break him down and get a confession.'

One could almost hear the A.C. muttering 'Here, here!'

'Chummie was there. That's the point to remember.'

'Yes, sir,' Canning urged. 'But does it really matter? Chummie may have been there, but if Hinton confesses, then chummie has to be in the clear.'

'But if he doesn't confess?'

'It's still a strong case, sir.'

Regretfully, Gently shook his head. In the absence of a confession, the proved presence of Cleeve would kill any case against Hinton stone dead.

'Can you really see Hinton wiping that gun and closing the dead man's fingers round it?'

'It's possible, sir.'

'It wasn't Hinton who rang us with a suicide theory that nearly fitted.'

'Perhaps some crank, sir . . . ?'

Gently hunched and went on staring at the register, lying open before him. Not Hinton: the Judge had had other thoughts when he slipped those cartridges into his gun. In some way, Cleeve had shown enough of his hand to put Pewsey on his guard: Pewsey had resolved to go armed to whatever rendezvous Cleeve had succeeded in fetching him to. Yet . . . how had Cleeve worked it? His behaviour at the Red Lion suggested that he had come there without a plan, ignorant of the lie of the land and needing even to check the Judge's address. So how? In a single morning, how set it all up?

The phone rang. Canning reached for it.

'Yes, sir . . . hold on.' He covered the mouthpiece. 'Someone at Erchildown, sir, wants to talk to the i/c of the case.'

Gently took the phone. 'Yes?'

'Am I speaking to the officer in charge?'

The voice sounded at once youthful and aggressive, and in the background one could hear confused murmurings.

'Speaking. What is your name?'

'My name is Mark Clevancy, and in case that means nothing to you I am Judge Pewsey's grandson. I'm phoning from the Cross Keys in Erchildown and I have important information, but it is essential that you hear it at the proper time and place.'

'What is your information, Mr Clevancy?'

'Sufficient for the moment that it is important.'

'Then if you will kindly call at Mazebridge Police Station—'

'No, officer. The place is here.'

Gently smothered an automatic reaction. 'If you could give me some indication . . . ?'

'Just meet me here at the Cross Keys, officer. I shall be here till half-past eight.'

Then the phone was hung up.

Slowly, Gently hung up at his end.

'Do we know if the Judge had a grandson by the name of Mark Clevancy?'

'Oh him, sir!' Canning made a face. 'He's a young so-and-so who drives a Morgan sports car. He often stays at the New Place and we've done him twice for motoring offences.'

'Now he is offering us information. But we have to go out there to collect it.'

'That sounds like him, sir. Shall I have him picked up?'

'We'll think about him—over a meal.'

5

A meal was brought to them in one of the booths that furnished the coffee-room at the Red Lion: a generous mixed grill followed by apple tart and cheese. Heywood had viewed their return with an apprehension which the handing back of his register had somewhat allayed; but then Gently had sparked it off afresh by requesting to book a room.

'I'm not sure—I think we're full up!'

'The register says three rooms are vacant.'

'Yes . . . but we're expecting people.'

'While I'm here I'm a "Mr Scott".'

The meal was served by a comely waitress who clearly wasn't fooled by any *nom de plume*, and Heywood's troubled face kept staring at them from the doorway. Finally he came across to the booth.

'Look . . . they're saying that this is connected with the shooting at Erchildown.'

'Who is saying?'

'Well—the staff, everyone! You see the Judge and Mrs Pewsey often came here.'

'Both the Judge and Mrs Pewsey?'

'Yes, of course! They often brought guests here for a meal. And now you come turning over a bedroom and going off with the hotel register . . .'

'Did Mrs Pewsey use to come here on her own?'

'I tell you they were both often here. Whenever they were in town they came here for coffee or a meal.'

'But Mrs Pewsey on her own?'

'Yes—sometimes!'

'She would meet her friends here—that sort of thing?'

'Exactly. So you see—'

'Was she by any chance here on Thursday?'

Poor Heywood! He had walked into it, and now he stood gazing pop-eyed at Gently. Canning, who had been quietly feeding himself Stilton, paused to stare interestedly at the manager.

'What you are suggesting is quite preposterous. She simply came here for tea. She had been shopping, I spoke to her. She left again directly afterwards.'

'But she was here—at the same time as "Mr Hamilton".'

'I insist, you're mistaken about that man! And in any case they were at separate tables, and had no communication. I was present during tea.'

'There was no exchange between them.'

'Utterly none.'

'Perhaps before they went in.'

'That wasn't possible. Mrs Pewsey was served at the commencement of tea, Mr Hamilton came down later.'

'And you have never seen them together on a previous occasion—someone she met here for coffee, or a drink?'

'Absolutely not.' But Heywood hesitated. 'She came in for coffee once with a gentleman, but I'm almost certain it wasn't the same man.'

'How long ago?'

'Oh . . . before Easter.'

'And you're "almost certain" it wasn't him?'

'Well, it was two months ago, but I'm pretty certain. And it's the only time I've seen her here with a gentleman.' Heywood had sunk his voice, and now he glanced over his shoulder. 'I trust . . . I hope . . . you're not suggesting any scandal. This hotel has always enjoyed the highest reputation.'

'In that case you can warn your staff to keep their mouths shut, especially to the press.'

'I will indeed. And in the meantime—'

'I'm a "Mr Scott", staying here on business.'

Heywood departed, and they saw him pause for an earnest word with the pretty waitress. Had they struck oil? At least it was a coincidence that Mrs Pewsey had been there on the

Thursday afternoon. A connection between her and 'Mr Hamilton' perhaps didn't quite fit with his occupations after dinner, but those may have had a different purpose. And if they had been acquainted as long ago as two months . . . ?

'Could have been something comic going on here, sir.'

Grunting, Gently carved himself some Stilton. On the face of it, nothing seemed more improbable than a liaison between Mrs Pewsey and the resurrected Cleeve! You would almost be forced to assume some earlier acquaintance, going back before his trial and conviction . . . and if there had been a relation between them then, would she since have married the man who had sent Cleeve to the gallows? Between that time and this had been an earlier marriage—but then, she would have supposed Cleeve dead.

'You say that young Clevancy often stayed with his grandfather?'

'Yes, sir. We did him for speeding only this Easter.'

'Perhaps he is worth another trip out to Erchildown.'

Canning said: 'I'll tell you one thing, sir. You'll get some cheek from him.'

Gently didn't hurry the drive. The downs were yellowing in the evening sun; yellowing too were the mounds of hawthorn through which the road to Erchildown took its lazy way. Trees, also gilded, fronted long shadows across the pastures and fields of hay, and even in the car you could smell the cow parsley that stood so lush and evening-still. Wiltshire: but it might have been Suffolk except for the sunny line of the downs. And over there, in the same late sunlight, wouldn't Gabrielle be just starting out on her evening stroll . . . ?

'Are you a local man?' Gently asked Canning.

'Me? Yes sir. Born in Mazey.'

'Where did you go to do your courting?'

'Well—up on the downs, sir!' Canning looked surprised. 'You can find a quiet spot up there.'

All the crescent of woods that enfolded Erchildown was

irradiated by sun as they dropped down to the village, but the village itself was in shade, except for the tower and spire of the church. A red Morgan 4/4 sports car stood parked before the half-timbered inn, and at an outside table a young man with ginger hair sat drinking with two girls.

'That's him, sir.'

'Fetch him here.'

Canning got out and approached the table. The young man greeted him mockingly, then slid his arm round the waist of one of the girls. Canning pointed to the car. The young man said something that set the girls laughing; finally he drank up his beer and swaggered across to Gently.

'Are you the officer I conversed with?'

'Just get in the car!' Gently snapped.

'But are you really the man in charge—a Chief Detective Superintendent, wasn't it?'

'If you have anything to say, get in the car.'

'Oh, I've plenty to say all right. But it must be to the right man in the right place—and in front of the right person.'

'Either you get in the car or stop wasting my time.'

'You can take it or leave it. But I've got the goods.'

Was he slightly drunk? There was a flush on his pugnacious, freckled features, about which the ginger hair bushed in a luxuriant, high-peaked style. He was wearing a plum-coloured sports shirt and wide-bottomed grey slacks, and had left a jacket hanging on his chair with what looked like a silk scarf. He had startingly blue eyes and spoke with a public-school accent.

'I'm a gift horse, did you know that? So you had better not look me in the mouth! I've driven over from Cambridge for your benefit, and in an hour from now I'll be driving back again. I shall top the ton here and there, to keep the rural gendarmes on their toes. You could give them a ring. They all know me. Tell them Clevancy rides again.'

'Is that supposed to be clever?'

'Heavens, no. Just small-talk to break the ice.'

'What do you know about the death of your grandfather?'

'Shot himself, didn't he? Or did he?'

Gently got out of the car, and Clevancy started back in mock terror. He was a strongly-built young man who looked as though he might go in for athletics, but stood most of a head shorter than Gently. The blue eyes had a sort of relishing gleam.

'How old are you, officer?'

Gently stared down at him.

'You know, I'm studying to be a barrister. One day quite soon, if you don't retire first, I may have the pleasure of meeting you in court. Won't that be an amusing moment—you in the box, and me asking the questions?'

'Only just at this moment, I'm asking them.'

'Oh, of course. And I'm a mere beginner.'

'You can start by telling me where you were on Friday.'

'That's the wrong question. It won't help a bit.'

'Still—suppose you answer it?'

Clevancy pretended a sigh. 'I always help the police—ask the Inspector. On Friday I had a run of free periods, so I trickled over to Bedford to see my sister. Though not entirely my sister, of course. Some of her college friends are rather ravishing. There's one called Claire—'

'Bedford is on the way here.'

'Ah. A point that should not be missed.'

'Did you come here?'

'I would love to say yes, but I'm stuck with this alibi at Bedford. You see, I can't very well get out of it—'

'Then precisely what do you have to tell me?'

'Nothing whatever, outside the Cross Keys. Can I buy you gentlemen a drink?'

He wasn't drunk, not even slightly; the gleam in his eyes testified to that. Up his sleeve a card was waiting to be played, and he was wringing every drop of satisfaction from it. Behind him the two girls were giggling, clearly adoring their young Lochinvar; while faces were peering from the pub doorway. Quite an evening entertainment for Erchildown!

'Very well then. Get in the drinks.'

But Clevancy remained eyeing him mischievously.

'You know, we don't have so very much time. I wouldn't want to be gated for the umpteenth occasion.'

'So what do you suggest?'

'Well . . . I dare say Angie will have finished dinner by now.'

'Angie?'

'Grandfather's second wife. Step-grandmother is a bit of a mouthful.'

'Are you suggesting a visit to her?'

Clevancy's eyes were tight. 'The right place, the right person, the right time.'

'Perhaps you should tell me what you have in mind, Mr Clevancy.'

'Yes—at the right place, before the right person, and at the right time.'

A stalemate! And both his eyes and his voice said that the young man wouldn't back down. This was his picnic and he was going to run it his way: otherwise the card would stay up his sleeve.

'You wish to give your information before Mrs Pewsey?'

'That's the only question I intend to answer.'

'It is something that affects her?'

He glanced at his watch. 'We've been talking here now for ten minutes.'

'She may not consent to see us.'

'Then I'm wasting my time. What did you say you would have to drink?'

Gently stared hard at Clevancy for some moments, then slowly shrugged.

'Very well! But if this is some game you are playing, it may not end up in the way you think.'

'Life is full of surprises, isn't it?' Clevancy couldn't keep the triumph out of his voice. 'My car or yours?'

'Drive your own,' Gently growled.

Clevancy went to fetch his jacket and to take a loving farewell of his two companions. Then he jumped into the red Morgan and catapulted away towards New Place. Gently's Rover followed at a more sedate pace. The Morgan vanished through the gates with puffs of tyre-smoke. When they arrived at the house, Clevancy was running up the steps to beat a tattoo with the elegant period knocker.

'Open up, Angie! It's your handsome step-grandson and two other charming people.'

His banging and shouting disturbed a wood-pigeon, sending it blundering off through the tree tops.

'Angie—yoo-hoo, Angie!'

After an interval, the door opened. Mrs Pewsey stood in the doorway, staring at Clevancy with smouldering eyes.

'You can turn straight round again, Mark, and drive back to wherever you came from.'

She was wearing the same black dress, but supplemented now by a lace fichu. Her hot eyes took in the two policemen then switched back to Clevancy; she stood barring his way, hand on door, ready to slam it.

'Angie, darling! Aren't you glad to see me?'

'I wonder you have the nerve to present yourself here.'

'But Angie dear, this is your Marco.'

'You will get back in your car and leave this minute.'

'Oh but Angie, I've brought these gentlemen. They're expecting to hear me tell you something interesting.'

'Then you can take them away again. You are obviously drunk, Mark, or you wouldn't have dared to intrude in this house.'

'I? Intrude in my grandfather's house? The house that one day is going to be mine?'

'You don't know that!'

'I know a lot of things, Angie. Hadn't you better let us in?'

She made a motion as though to slam the door, but then froze again, glaring. The whole tense little scene was being strangely punctuated by the continuous evening birdsong. The house was in shade; above it, the tree tops were bathed in the level sun, sun lay along the lake, the sounds of evening were rounded and clear.

'What about it, Angie?'

'You don't cross this threshold!'

'Shall I shout what I know for the servants to hear?'

'You are drunk, and you have come to make trouble. I wonder that the police are here encouraging you.'

'Hold it!' Gently interrupted. He mounted the steps and placed a hand on Clevancy's arm. 'Either Mrs Pewsey allows us in, or you are going to tell me your tale in another place.'

Clevancy shook his head. 'It's here or nowhere.'

'If you carry on like this it could be the Police Station.'

'Then it's up to Angie.'

Gently looked at Mrs Pewsey, whose hazel eyes flared back at his.

'Oh, let the drunken lout have his say.'

'It is entirely your decision, Mrs Pewsey.'

'If he can bear tales, then so can I.'

She stepped back to allow them in.

At the rear of the hall, below the handsome staircase, hung a painting of the Judge by Augustus John, a three-quarter-length portrait showing Pewsey enveloped in a crimson gown with white cuffs. His sharp features were enveloped by the wig and gazed down sternly at the beholder; John had caught the accusing quality of the eyes, a pitiless set in the thin lips. To this painting Clevancy marched; he spent several moments silently before it. Finally he turned from it and struck a pose, his hand grasping his lapel.

'Let me lay the ground, as we lawyers say! My grandfather was quite a wealthy man. Besides this property and two farms he had investments of over half a million. He leaves two daughters, the eldest my mother, and I am the only male heir. So when my grandfather dies in mysterious circumstances, I may be said to have an interest.'

'What would you know about your interest!' Mrs Pewsey snapped. 'At Easter, Arthur threw you out of the house.'

Clevancy nodded. 'Point taken. But I happen to have read a very interesting document.'

'If you are referring to his will, that is impossible, because it is deposited with his solicitor.'

'The will is, but there's a copy. And that is in the safe in grandfather's study.'

'How do you know that?'

'Let's say that I do. Let's say that one day grandfather was careless. And the will tells me that the property goes to you for your lifetime, after which it reverts to me.'

'That's all you know about it, my son!' Mrs Pewsey was fuming. 'The copy you saw is that of a will that Arthur made when we were married. He's changed it since, you didn't know that, I doubt if you figure in it now. He saw his solicitor after Easter, and you know full well what happened then.'

'Grandfather changed his will after Easter?'

'Yes, so you can forget your dreams of owning this place.'

'But he did change it?'

'Oh, he changed it.'

'That was what I wished to know, Angie.'

Something in his voice pulled her up short, and she hesitated, her eyes fierce. Then she exclaimed: 'And much good may it do you! It didn't need the police brought here for that.'

'Still laying the ground. Now we have it on the table that grandfather changed his will after Easter. The next consideration is why? What happened at Easter to provide a motive?'

'Do you really want me to tell them?'

Clevancy shook his head. 'This is where your Marco provides some testimony. About his movements. On the Good Friday. On the afternoon when he arrived here.'

'And what can you mean by that?'

'I mean I arrived to find the place deserted. Grandfather had gone into town with Alton, Mrs Alton and Sarah had gone with him, and your car was missing from the garage. There was only the horse looking after the place. Well, it wasn't much of a reception on a fine afternoon, and after kicking my heels for a while I decided to go for a tramp on the downs.'

Now Mrs Pewsey had gone very still. Clevancy had hold of both his lapels; he wasn't looking at Mrs Pewsey but staring at some point above their heads.

'I went up the Coate Hill and along the tops as far as the beacon, then I came down by Wellbottom tumulus to join the road by Wellbottom Lane. At the top of the lane I found two cars parked, one of them Angie's green Lancia. I went to look for her in the little beech wood that has grown up round the tumulus. I found her. I found her with a man. They were in a situation I didn't care to disturb. So I left them to it and returned to the house to have a few words with the horse.'

'You liar—you scandalous liar!' Mrs Pewsey had gone deathly white. 'This is your revenge, isn't it, for me shopping you to Arthur! Well, it won't do, my fine fellow. That afternoon I was nowhere near Wellbottom. As it happens I drove into Bath, that's where I spent Good Friday afternoon.'

'But can you prove it, Angie?'

'I don't have to prove it. It isn't me telling scandalous lies. On the other hand *I* can provide some testimony—that Arthur's grandson was guilty of attempted rape!'

Clevancy clicked his tongue. 'Not rape. I confess to a little misguided ardour.'

'Rape. You tore my clothes. I had to bloody your nose to keep you off.'

'Well, you must admit the way seemed clear. After what I had seen in Wellbottom Wood.'

'You saw nothing there, or if you did you were watching some other woman than me.'

'Your car, Angie.'

'My car was in Bath.'

'And I'm asking you again—can you prove it?'

'You malignant devil.'

She was breathing quickly, her hands clenched at her sides. Clevancy had a tremulous sneer on his lips; you felt he hadn't quite finished yet.

'And this—this abominable lie you retailed to Arthur?'

'Perhaps not quite in so many words. But when he was

representing my iniquity to me so eloquently, I felt obliged to enter grounds of diminished culpability.'

'You told him!'

'I told him your accusation was on a par with the pot calling the kettle black. It seemed to strike him. He came over thoughtful, and you can make what you like of that.'

'You killed him. You killed Arthur.'

'I? Did someone kill him?'

'Yes—you. With that filthy lie. But for that, he would still be alive today.'

'But it wasn't a lie, Angie. And grandfather seemed to know it. So putting it all together, how exactly did grandfather die?'

Her fingers were hooking out towards him. 'Get out, get out of here, Mark Clevancy! And don't dare come back, ever, not you, nor your sister, nor your insinuating mother. And you can tell them why, because you killed your grandfather with the wickedest lie ever told. Now, not another word from you—get out of this house and my life for ever!'

'Well done, Angie!'

'Get out.'

'Just a moment!' Gently broke in. 'With regard to the man you claim to have seen, Mr Clevancy, perhaps you can offer us a description?'

'He can't,' Mrs Pewsey spat. 'Because he never saw one.'

Clevancy shrugged. 'I have to admit that I can't describe him. He—ah—had his back to me when I had him under observation.'

'You see!'

'But the car?' Gently said.

'Oh yes. I can offer a description of that. It was a beige Vauxhall Cavalier with tan upholstery and spoked wheel trims.'

'Of course you wouldn't have the number?'

'But yes.' Clevancy drew a notebook from his pocket. 'Here we are—a local registration.' He tore out a page and handed it to Gently.

'Oh, you devil!' Mrs Pewsey gasped

Clevancy inclined his head. 'I think that concludes my business, officer. And now I must be getting back to coll.'

He went, closing the door behind him almost without a sound; moments later they heard the growl of the Morgan, a shatter of gravel, and the sound of the engine peak and die away.

'He was lying of course. That was his revenge for my complaining about him to Arthur. He is an animal, a vicious animal. He forced Sarah too, but she wouldn't complain.'

Mrs Pewsey's mouth was bitter, her determined chin thrust high. She was confronting Gently, feet straddled, defiance in her every line.

'I'm afraid we shall have to check this number.'

'Oh, it will be the car of someone we know. Mark wouldn't miss a trick like that, it will perhaps be someone he wants to make trouble for.'

'Someone you know?'

'That would follow, wouldn't it? Not only a lie, but a lie with a circumstance. A fine lawyer Mark Clevancy will turn out—a mouthpiece for criminals, as like as not.'

'Please look at this number.'

'What is it to me? I can barely remember my own.'

'It would save us time and trouble if you could recognise it, along with the description he gave of the car.'

'Oh, very well.' She glanced at the number, her mouth even more sour than before. She jerked her head. 'I suppose it is quite pointless to ask you not to go bothering this man?'

'Then you do know who it is?'

Her head jerked again. 'Mark could scarcely have chosen better. He has put you on to a man that I knew when I was young, but who I met again only recently.'

'How recently?'

'Two months ago. He had been out of the country for years. I happened to recognise him in Mazebridge High Street and since then we have renewed the acquaintance. But that's all. He isn't my lover, except in Mark's ingenious brain. I suppose Mark saw me with him somewhere and his nasty little mind jumped to conclusions.'

Her eyes were hard on Gently's, her voice vibrant, her snub-nosed face pushing towards him.

'And—he's been living abroad?'

'Didn't I say so? He came back to England two years ago. His wife left him, taking their children, and he decided to come back here.'

'Where had he been living, Mrs Pewsey?'

'Rhodesia. Zimbabwe, the blacks now call it.'

'Do you know for how long?'

'Thirty years at least. I was only a girl when he left England.'

'Thirty years.'

'Give or take. During which time I've been married twice.'

How much was she lying? In her own defence she would probably twist the truth without conscience; and Clevancy would hardly have taken the car number unless he had seen conduct more flagrant than she was admitting.

'This man was known to the Judge too?'

'Of course. I had no need to hide him from Arthur.'

But Pewsey was dead.

'When did you last see him?'

'Oh . . . in Mazebridge, one day last week.'

'On Thursday, perhaps?'

'I was certainly in town then, collecting some bottles for the evening.'

'You met him in the Red Lion?'

She checked, her eyes cautious. 'No. I ran across him in the street.'

'And that is the last time you have seen him?'

'Good lord yes. I've told you, he is simply a casual acquaintance. I saw a lot of him in the old days, but that has all changed. Now he's almost a stranger.'

'Where were those old days spent?'

'What? We both lived at Prior's Compton.'

'And he left there for Zimbabwe thirty years ago?'

'If it matters, around then.'

'Not nearer twenty—say eighteen?'

Was she acting the incomprehension in her eyes?

'I haven't an idea what you are getting at, but the answer is no. He went out in the early 'fifties, I can't be positive when, to join his family, who were farming there. I really can't see the point of these questions.'

'And he knew you previously, but not the Judge.'

'Can I put it any plainer?'

'This afternoon, were you expecting a visit from him?'

She flushed up, her eyes sparkling.

'This is the end. If you believe Mark's lies, then you are less intelligent than I thought you. You have seen him; he is vindictive and clever, and has a motive for giving me trouble. So believe him if you want to, but I shall answer no more questions.'

'A final one, Mrs Pewsey. You were going to assist me with this man's name.'

Snatching her head away, she snapped: 'if you must know, his name is Jonathan Stoke.'

'And his address?'

'High-and-Low Farm, Clyffe. Now kindly remove yourselves from my house.'

They went, and she slammed the door after them, setting the wood-pigeon off again.

Canning said: 'Do we go after this boyo, sir?'

'Yes,' Gently said. 'We go after him.'

6

A quarter of a mile beyond the New Place gates the minor road made its departure southward, at first through a spur of the woodland, then descending by the warren into open country. Canning pointed out the gap where Pewsey had left his car, the junction of the lane, and Hinton's cottage, the latter just visible among trees and reached by a farm-road on their left; lastly, a mile further on, he indicated a line of hawthorns that ended in a shadowy grove.

'Wellbottom Tumulus, sir.'

Gently eased the Rover as they approached it. The hawthorns overhung a narrow lane that wriggled its way into the downs. Low sun was reddening the fan of beeches and the shoulder of downs behind it, on the summit of which stood a stone pillar, doubtless the beacon mentioned by Clevancy.

'A likely spot I'd say, sir. And it lies on the right road.'

But if Clevancy had invented his tale, he was shrewd enough to have chosen a plausible setting.

'One of them is lying.'

'My money's on the lady, sir. Chummie we have seen up this way ourselves.'

'If it was him.'

'I'd be surprised if it wasn't, sir, and it does fit in with Hinton's story. Then there's what happened at the Red Lion on Thursday.'

'By all accounts, not very much!'

'But it keeps adding up, sir. If this chummie is the boyfriend, and he was parked in the lane when the Judge was shot.'

Gently grunted and speeded up again. The road led through a cleft in the high downs. Shortly they could see spread below them a broad vale where the westering sun lit a glimmer of water. Beyond lay another ridge of the downs, here and there smudged by belts of trees, and clustering at the river a group of stonebuilt houses and a hogback bridge with a pepper-pot tollhouse. The sun, slipping now into horizon clouds, laid a rosy light on the scene, giving a tinge of pink to grey-yellow stonework reflected in the unrippled river.

'Seven miles from the New Place. Is there a direct road to Mazebridge?'

'Yes sir. Clyffe is eight miles from town, on a through road to Amesbury.'

They crossed the bridge and entered a square where cars were parked around a market cross. Gently halted while Canning sought direction; the farm was distant from the village. A main road took them to a by-road, the by-road to a lane, then at last they were approaching an old stone farmhouse about which stood horse-chestnuts in ghostly bloom. Before it spread a rutted sweep along one side of which ranged an open cart-lodge; and there, among tractors and farm machinery, was parked a beige Cavalier with spoked wheel trims. Off left stood a farm cottage from a chimney of which the smoke rose straight, but nothing else was stirring as the Rover homed in.

'He may have cleared off, sir,' Canning muttered. 'The lady is bound to have given him a buzz.'

They got out, and Gently rapped firmly on a panelled door on which paint was blistering. From the downs behind the house they could hear sheep bleating, but no movement from within. He rapped again: and this time was answered by a sudden tumult of barking. A collie dog came racing round the house to crouch angry-eyed in front of him.

'Yes—you were looking for me?'

A man had followed the dog. He was wearing breeches and green derriboots and an old tweed jacket over a twill shirt. His age was about fifty, his height was six feet. And there was a certain flattening of the vowels in his speech.

'You are Jonathan Stoke?'

'Yes, that's me.'

Wary, warm-brown eyes met Gently's. The face was young-old, haggard featured, the greyed hair wiry with a hint of curl. The features of the photograph? It wasn't impossible: this was a face that had seen suffering. Such a one might well have been Cleeve's, eighteen years after his brush with the hangman.

'We are policemen. We are enquiring into the death of Judge Pewsey. We have reason to believe that you may be able to help us.'

'I help you? But how?'

'On Friday, a car resembling yours was seen in the neighbourhood of the Judge's house.'

'Resembling mine . . . ?'

'Also, a man said to resemble yourself.'

'But . . . on Friday . . .'

'Shall we go inside, Mr Stoke?'

He was alarmed, no question about that: it was plain from his horrified stare. Yet after a pause he pulled himself together and, with a word to the dog, led them into the house. They went through a flagged hall into a low-ceilinged lounge, a dank room that smelt of mould and was drably furnished in 'thirties style. New were a television set and a Magicoal electric fire: the rest had probably come with the house. Stoke hesitated, then pointed to chairs.

'I honestly don't know what to say . . .'

'Have you a British passport, Mr Stoke?'

'Yes, of course. But what—?'

'I would be obliged if you would produce it.'

His stare was baffled. 'But—look here! That wasn't what you said you'd come about.'

'Have you any objection to producing it?'

'Yes, I have. First I would want to know why.'

He felt for a chair, and sat stiffly, the collie coming to squat at his feet. He bent to give it a pat, at the same time staring up at Gently.

'I'm British. I always have been. I never even put in for dual nationality. When I came back here do you think they didn't check? Get on to the immigration people—they'll soon tell you.'

'How long were you abroad, Mr Stoke?'

'I don't see what that has to do with it, either.'

'Do you mind telling me?'

'No, I don't. But I just can't see how it's any of your business.'

'Take it that it is.'

'So then I'll tell you. I was out of the country for twenty-eight years.'

'Not eighteen?'

'Twenty-eight. And if that's a crime, I would like to know how.'

He went on patting the dog, which gazed into his face and gave little whines. Apart from the flat vowels he had a cultivated voice that seemed somehow out of keeping with his clothes and the room. A bookcase in a corner was full of newish books and others were stacked on a table. On the walls hung framed maps, one of Africa; and a framed photograph of a group of African natives.

'What year did you leave England?'

'Does it matter?'

'What made you choose Rhodesia?'

He fondled the dog's ears. 'There's something funny about all this! If I've broken some regulation, perhaps you'll just tell me. But I'm here, and I'm legitimate, and it has nothing to do with a judge getting shot.'

'Nothing?'

'Exactly nothing. Just tell me where there is a connection. I only ever met the Judge once, and that certainly wasn't in the bush.'

'Then where did you meet him?'

'Not in Rhodesia. I went there for family reasons.'

'What family reasons?'

Stoke's eyes were blank. 'My family went out there farming, didn't they?'

Gently stared hard at him. 'Did they?'

'Yes, they did. So what about it?'

'And they are still there?'

'Yes, they are still there. Except my father and my uncle, who are dead.' He went on stroking. 'This is bloody stupid. Because what have my family got to do with your job? They didn't know the Judge either, nor make a habit of shooting people. I've got a married sister out there, and my mother lives with her. Then there's my son, Peter, who's in government service. And my daughter, who's still at college, and an ex-wife. That's the lot.'

'Just you alone who returned to England.'

'What's so strange about that? I was left alone there, running the farm. The others had gone to live in S.A. I lost the kids when my wife left me, then my mother went too. And I fancied England more than S.A., so I sold up the farm and came back here.'

'It makes an interesting story. And if I should want to get in touch with your relatives?'

Stoke gazed up at him. 'Just go to hell,' he said.

'Let's go back to before you left England. Where do you say you were living then?'

The collie had gone to stretch out by the hearth, nose on paws, but with wide open eyes. Stoke was sitting up straight, his expression tense, eyes narrowed to face Gently. Outside the light was fading and the room was becoming shadowy.

'Look, what is the sense of all this? If you really do have business, suppose we get down to it.'

'Weren't you, for example, living in Sussex?'

'No! I never have lived in Sussex.'

'Then where?'

'Oh lord. Before I left England, I was a student at Southampton University.'

'A student?'

'Yes, a bloody student. Try to prove something different. It'll be down there in their records if they keep them that far back.'

'The name, Jonathan Stoke.'

'Right. Studying geography and agricultural science. Home address, Smallwood Farm, Prior's Compton. Previous school, Prior's Compton Grammar.'

'You remember it readily.'

'Why shouldn't I? Jonathan Stoke happens to be me.'

'And his family, your family?'

Stoke checked. 'What are you trying to get at now?'

Gently said: 'Let's take a case, the case of a man who wants to change his identity, who has good reason for wanting to leave the country, who needs a passport, preferably authentic. Do you know how he gets it?'

'Why the hell would I?'

'He gets it like this,' Gently said. 'First, he checks the mortality columns of the newspapers for a person of about the same age as himself, then he applies for a copy of that person's birth certificate. Using the certificate, photographs of himself, and a form bearing a faked referee's signature, he applies for a passport, and most usually he gets one. Then he is equipped with an identity proof against any common form of enquiry.'

Stoke's eyes were wide. 'But this is crazy. Are you saying I did that?'

'I'm putting a case,' Gently said. 'This is one way identities are faked. Unfortunately there is a drawback. The person whose identity is borrowed is dead, and if suspicion should arise his death is an easy matter to prove. Thus there may be a Jonathan Stoke who studied at Southampton University and whose family emigrated from Prior's Compton, but not a Jonathan Stoke who was in any situation to follow them.'

Stoke started up. 'And you really believe—!'

'Do you have a copy of your birth certificate, Mr Stoke?'

His eyes stared wildly. 'I think I must be going mad! If I'm not me, then who am I? Who was I before I went to Africa? Who does my mother think I am—my two children, my ex-wife?'

'Please be calm, Mr Stoke.'

'But you are trying to steal my very identity! Heaven knows I don't have much, but I felt I could be certain of that. I've lost my wife, lost my children, can't look my bank manager in the face, but I'm still Jonathan Stoke, whatever you are trying to insinuate.'

'Then may I see your birth certificate and passport?'

'Suppose I told you I had lost them.'

'Have you lost them?'

'No, I haven't. But where would I be if I had?'

'Then you can produce them.'

'I can if I choose. But they are in my safe deposit at Maze-bridge. And that's where they are going to stay, unless you give me a very good reason.'

'It may come to my holding you in custody until your identity can be proved.'

'You can't do that. And if you could, you could only prove I am who I say.'

'Would you object to your fingerprints being taken?'

'My fingerprints!' Now there was real alarm in his eyes. 'But they're not on record—why should you want them? I haven't done anything criminal.'

'You refuse?'

'Yes, I refuse.

'I may also request you to take part in an identity parade.'

'An identity parade.' He dropped back on his chair. 'Now we are really coming to it, aren't we?'

As though made uneasy by its master's distress the collie came to lay its head on Stoke's knee, gazing up at him with protruding bright eyes and giving small, consoling whines. It was a black-and-white bitch with a bushy tail that swept weakly to and fro. Stoke patted its neck, ran his fingers round its ears. The bitch quieted; she looked round at Gently, then snuggled closer to Stoke's thigh.

'Who put you on to me anyway?'

'Has no one rung you in the past hour?'

'How could they? I've been seeing to stock. I had only just come down from the pasture.'

'Someone took the number of your car.'

Stoke stared, but said nothing.

'This afternoon you were seen near Erchildown Old Place, where your car was parked in the lane.'

'No.'

'You had left your car. You were proceeding towards the New Place. Then you were disturbed. You ran back to your car and drove off in this direction. What were you doing there, Mr Stoke?'

'I—nothing!' His hand on the dog trembled. 'I deny it, I wasn't at Erchildown. Someone must have made a mistake.'

'You weren't there on a visit?'

'No. I scarcely know Mrs Pewsey.'

'Your car and hers were seen parked together at Wellbottom Tumulus on another occasion.'

'That's not possible.'

'The day was Good Friday.'

'I . . . on Good Friday I was out somewhere. Yes, I remember now. I had some business in Salisbury.'

'Yet surely you know Mrs Pewsey quite well?'

'No . . . at least, only to speak to.'

'According to her there was a previous acquaintance, when you were both quite young.'

'Oh—then.' He was striving for composure, his face turned to the dog. 'Yes, but that was a long time ago. It has been a lifetime since then.'

'Yet you recognised each other when you met?'

'Yes . . . I think it was her who recognised me. We . . . it was the first time for thirty years. Of course, we had a few things to tell each other.'

'That would have been at the Red Lion at Mazebridge.'

'I'd like to know who's been telling you all this! If it matters, we went in there for coffee and stopped to have a chat. After all, we went to school together, Angela was a friend of my sister's. We kept saddle-horses at the farm and she often came over to ride with us. Then her family were solicitors who took care of all our business . . . we lived in and out of each other's pockets! So why shouldn't we have things to talk about?'

'And after that . . . other meetings?'

'Yes, I saw her once or twice in Mazebridge. I go there to market, and people usually come to town on Saturdays.'

'But not only at Mazebridge?'

'What are you hinting at?'

'We have different information, Mr Stoke. It says your relations, with Mrs Pewsey went much closer than mere acquaintance.'

'That isn't true!'

'It relates to Good Friday.'

'But that . . . I told you . . . I went to Salisbury.'

'To an incident between you at Wellbottom Tumulus.'

Stoke gulped, his eyes fearful.

'So why were you at Erchildown this afternoon?'

'I—I was nowhere near Erchildown.'

'But on Friday afternoon you were there. Your car was parked in the lane, and you were seen coming out of the summerhouse.'

Stoke's eyes rolled at Gently, and his mouth trembled wretchedly.

'I deny that, and everything you've put to me!'

It had taken Stoke a few moments to get control of himself. At a signal from Gently, Canning had switched on the lights, but they glowed feebly from parchment shades. The room looked shabbier, Stoke's face more haggard; and the collie was whining incessantly. Attracted by the light, moths tappped at the window, their tiny eyes points of fire.

'You said you had met the Judge. When was that?'

One could almost feel Stoke stiffen.

'Actually . . . that is to say, I saw him once with his wife, in Mazebridge.'

'But before that?'

'No, I'd never met him. Nor was I introduced to him then.'

'But earlier still?'

'How could I? Once and for all, the answer is no.'

He was in a state when it was nearly impossible to guess whether he was telling a lie or the truth, the one sounding like the other; while his eyes had a sullen, desperate appearance.

'We'll leave that. What I want from you now is an account of your movements on Thursday and Friday.'

'I was minding my business—'

'Wait. I may already have information.'

Stoke flinched. 'I never left the farm, not on the Thursday that is. You can ask Langley at the cottage. I'm not exactly a man of leisure.'

'So you couldn't have been seen in Mazebridge?'

'No, I couldn't.'

'At the Red Lion?'

He didn't reply.

'But on Thursday you perhaps had callers? A conversation on the phone?'

His eyes sank to the collie. 'There were no callers. I may have talked on the phone. A customer who's taking some lambs, my feed merchant in town.'

'No private calls?'

His mouth was tight.

'I suggest a conversation with Mrs Pewsey.'

'You can suggest all you like.'

'Let's come to Friday, then.'

Stoke swallowed. 'On Friday . . . Friday morning I went into town. I had some business there with the bank—Lloyds Bank, you can ask them.'

'How long did that take?'

'I don't know! I had an appointment for eleven. When I came out I did some shopping and picked up a filter for the Fordson tractor.'

'Go on.'

'Well . . . then it was latish, half-past twelve, getting on for one. So I thought I might as well eat in town, and I had my lunch at the Red Lion.'

'At half-past twelve.'

'Say nearer one . . . later, by the time I was served. I wasn't in a hurry, I took my time, read a *Farmers' Weekly* I'd just bought.'

'And you left when?'

'I can't be precise! It could have been as late as three . . . but I was back here by half-past, Langley can verify that. He was waiting for me, wanted to know which pasture we were moving the flock to.'

'You went for lunch at twelve-thirty and arrived back here three hours later?'

'Yes, I suppose so! I told you, I didn't hurry over lunch.'

'Which way did you come?'

'Well naturally . . . I came here straight from Mazebridge.'

'Not by Erchildown?'

'Why should I, when it puts four miles on the trip?'

'Yet you were seen at Erchildown.'

Stoke's mouth quivered. 'Somebody is making a mistake.'

'At approximately ten minutes to three you were seen to leave Judge Pewsey's summerhouse.'

'But I don't know the summerhouse! I've never been there.'

'You went to your car, parked in the lane. You were seen driving off towards Clyffe, where you would have arrived in time to speak to your employee at three-thirty.'

'I can't help it, it simply isn't true, I wasn't near Erchildown on Friday.'

'And you spent three hours over lunch?'

'Not three hours! It was more like two—'

'But even two?'

'Yes, two . . . it was afterwards I collected the filter from the garage.'

'Perhaps it was then you did the rest of your shopping?'

'Yes, perhaps . . . I don't remember.'

'I put it to you, Mr Stoke, that you did drive to Erchildown, and that you were the man seen leaving the summerhouse shortly after Judge Pewsey was shot.'

'I deny it, I utterly deny it, my movements were those I've given you.'

'Yet you refuse to take part in an identity parade?'

'Yes. Yes—I refuse!'

'And to having your fingerprints taken?'

'Oh God. Merciful God.'

He put out his arms to the whining collie, who at once sprang on his lap. He hugged the collie. She licked his face with eager, nervous, affectionate movements. Could they have broken him? His story was as leaky as a sieve: it needed only someone at the Red Lion to remember at what time he had left there on Friday. Canning was eyeing Stoke with a hawkish glee: no question what the local man was thinking. And whenever fingerprints were mentioned . . . couldn't that lined face once have been Cleeve's?

'Tomorrow, the bank opens at nine-thirty. I want to see you at the Police Station at ten. You will bring your passport and birth certificate and I shall require a statement from you.'

'But that, that's all nonsense—'

'You had better understand that I shall be checking what you have told me. So think it over carefully before you make your statement tomorrow.'

'I've told you the truth!'

Gently stared at him. Stoke hugged the collie tighter.

'One more question.'

Fear was in his eyes.

'Isn't your brother still living in England?'

'My brother?' The eyes went blank. 'But I never had a brother.'

'Your twin brother.'

'But I'm not a twin, and I've only a sister in S.A.'

Gently held his gaze for a moment.

'Then tomorrow at ten, Mr Stoke.'

They drove in silence to the village, where lights in the pubs now shone brightly, and where people loitered on the bridge or along a walk beside the river. Canning had once or twice glanced at Gently, but Gently had ignored him; finally, as they slowed at junction, Canning could contain himself no longer.

'Sir, I don't know about you, but for my money that man is both our chummie and yours!'

Gently went through the gears before replying: 'One thing is certain . . . he isn't "Mr Hamilton".'

'Oh, that fellow.' Canning sounded derisive. 'I'd say that was all my eye. The man left the hotel in a hurry, and Heywood fancied he looked like the photograph. But Stoke is different. He's got it all going for him. I reckon he's a classic case.'

'Is that how you see it?'

'Yes I do, sir.' Canning hitched round in his seat. 'Look, there's this lady with a rich, elderly husband, who runs into a Romeo from her past. But though the old boy is elderly, he's tough, has maybe fifteen years left in him, and what's more he has sussed out something that makes him think of changing his will. So he has to go, and in his case a shooting accident is the perfect answer. He's seventy-eight, always out with a gun, nobody will give it a moment's thought. They kid him along that if he goes to the summerhouse he's going to catch them at it, but what he finds there is Stoke with the gun, which the lady has provided. Then bang, bang—wipe the gun, and the rest is up to the lady.'

Gently shrugged. 'Ingenious.'

'Yes sir, but a couple of things they didn't allow for—Hinton's being in the warren, and chummie leaving a dab that we could identify. I'd say that was the reason for the phone call, them getting worried about what we were up to. It seemed we weren't going to buy an accident, so they came in with the suicide bit.'

'And if Stoke shouldn't happen to be my chummie?'

'He has to be, sir, as I see it.'

'His account of himself squares with the lady's.'

'Yes sir, but it would do, wouldn't it? She knows who he really is, so they've invented this story of his past between them. But that will fall flat on its face the moment we get hold of his dabs.'

'Yes . . . his dabs.'

'They really bother him, sir. He was getting screwed up whenever you mentioned them.'

'Yet as far as he knows they are off record.'

'Which leaves only one answer, doesn't it, sir?'

One answer: that Stoke was sweating in case he had failed to clean up at the summerhouse, had made some mistake in those terrifying minutes that followed the discharge of the gun. Could it be that he remembered, too late, having seized hold of the door knob, as he rushed in a panic from the scene of his crime?

'Tomorrow, I want Hinton brought in and detained in a car outside the Police Station. He isn't to be briefed. If he recognises Stoke, I want an officer able to swear that recognition was voluntary.'

'Yes, sir. I'll take care of it.'

'Do we know who Pewsey's solicitors were?'

'Yes, sir, Shaw and Atworth.'

'I'd like to know if there really was a new will and how it differs from its predecessor.'

Canning made a face. 'That might be tricky, sir.'

'Do the best you can with it. Meanwhile we'll pick up a photofit kit and see what Heywood can make with it.'

Dinner was still in progress when they arrived at the Red Lion, and Heywood was in haste to sweep the policemen into his office. Impatiently, he listened to Canning's instructions as the photofit kit was spread out on the desk.

'Really, couldn't this have waited? You choose the most inconvenient times!'

Gently said: 'Would you have been present during lunch on Friday, Mr Heywood?'

'No I wasn't, I had a wholesaler in. What has Friday lunch got to do with it?'

'I would like to talk to someone who was serving table at that meal.'

Still protesting, Heywood summoned the pretty waitress, whose name was Eileen. At first confused, she remembered eventually that one of Friday's customers was reading a magazine.

'A man of about fifty, with strongly marked features?'

'He was one of the first in here. Sat at a single table, reading all the way through the meal.'

'Do you know when he left?'

'Ah, now. He had gone by the time we finished serving.'

'When was that?'

'Two o'clock. And he left me a tip . . . fifty pence.'

Heywood's picture, when it was done, bore some slight resemblance to Stoke, but approximated much more nearly to the photographs of Cleeve. Had it been a fair attempt, or had the photographs influenced Heywood? Eileen, who had waited on 'Hamilton', testified to the likeness.

'Have it copied and circulated.'

'Right you are, sir.'

And that was that, for one day.

After treating Canning to a drink, Gently retired to ring Gabrielle. The new curtains were up, she told him, and made their bedroom look quite different, while on her walk down the little valley she had listened to the nightingale for all of ten minutes.

'But it needed you there, my dear. I think that nightingale sounded lonely. Where is this Wiltshire?'

'In the West Country.'

'Aha. But it is not Suffolk.'

After Normandy, in Gabrielle's book, Suffolk was the true land of Cockaigne.

7

Gently woke in his bedroom at the Red Lion with an odd sensation that he had 'gone foreign', and that the traffic he could hear stirring below his window was that of some small French town, Scottish at least.

He got up and pulled his curtains. Sun came pouring in to dazzle him. Below, a few vehicles were moving in the High Street and one or two early-risers stepping out along the pavements, while across the way a man with a pole was hauling down the sunblinds of an ironmonger's shop.

But that was the foreground; spreading behind it, seen over the roofs of shadowy stone buildings, was the pastelled line of the downs with the White Horse pinned to them like a brooch. And somehow he found them disturbing, if not foreign then in some way remote: on a different plane. He lit his pipe and remained staring for several minutes.

Breakfast, a meal seemingly intended to last for the whole day, was served in the booths of the coffee-lounge, and it was there that Canning joined him, in time for a cup of coffee.

'I've just come from the solicitor's, sir.'

There was matter in Canning's blue eyes.

'The bosses hadn't arrived, but I talked to the clerk and got some information out of him. There was a new will all right. The Judge called in there a few days after Easter. According to the clerk some major changes were involved, though of course he wouldn't tell me what. But the will wasn't signed, they were still preparing it, so it won't be produced. And they won't tell us what was in it in case it prejudices their client, Mrs Pewsey.' Canning winked. 'Good enough, sir?'

'Good enough,' Gently grunted.

'So now we know, sir. The Judge had to go, and they didn't

have a lot of time. I reckon the lady gave away she knew the will wasn't signed when she was rowing with young Clevancy, because otherwise she'd have kept quiet about it. But she knew we could never get to see it.'

Because Mrs Pewsey was now the client, the estate, two farms and half a million. If one thing was certain it was that the new draft will had already gone through the office shredder. And they couldn't prove it had ever existed: that clerk wouldn't be standing up in court.

'Anything else?'

'Yes, sir. Mason and Bridges are the only Fordson agents in town, so I looked in there. It was around noon on Friday when Stoke picked up the filter.'

'Have you brought in Hinton?'

'I told him we wanted him to amend his statement, sir. I've got him parked next to the steps with my sergeant keeping him company.' Canning glanced at his watch. 'Do you reckon we'll have him, sir?'

'We shall if he's the man who left the dab.'

'But even if he isn't?'

Gently shrugged: in that case, they would need to break him to make it stick.

'Let's go.'

Outside the Police Station stood the patrol car with Hinton sitting in it. Catching sight of Gently, he struggled to get out, but was pinned down by the man sitting with him. They found Pypard in his office. He was scribbling something on a pad, but jumped up excitedly as they entered.

'That chummie of yours! He's been at it again. I've only just put down the phone.'

'You mean Stoke?'

'He didn't say, did he? Now he's on about a bloke called Cleeve.'

Automatically, Gently checked his watch; the time was five-and-twenty to ten. By now, if he were following instructions, Stoke should be inside the bank, collecting his documents.

'Get me Lloyds Bank on the phone.'

'Yes, but chummie's ringing up isn't all—!'

'Get them.'

Indignantly, Pypard found the number, rang, and handed the phone to Gently.

'Police Station. Is a customer of yours, Mr Stoke, on the premises?'

'Hold on a minute, sir . . . yes, he's here. Did you want to speak to him?'

'When did he come in?'

'Just this moment, sir. Actually, he's gone down into the vaults . . .'

'Thank you, that's all.'

Gently handed back the phone.

'It could have been him, sir,' Canning urged.

'Yes . . . it could have been.'

'But, look here, sir!' Pypard broke in. 'That phone has been hot ever since I came in. First it was an earful from Mrs Pewsey, threatening to sue us for slanderous allegations, then a tearing off by the Chief Constable, who happens to be a pal of hers, more or less telling me to drop the case. And now chummie again. And yesterday we just about had this thing sewn up . . . !'

'You made notes of that conversation?'

'I was making them, sir.'

'Let's hear what chummie had to say.'

'Well, he mentioned this name, sir, Eric Trevor Cleeve, and said that he was what it was all about. Is Cleeve the name of your chummie, sir?'

'Just get on.'

Pypard hesitated, his dark eyes keen. 'It fits what you were telling us, sir, that Cleeve was a bloke who the Judge sent for the chop. Said Cleeve was innocent, and the Judge knew it, that it had preyed on his mind for years, that recently the Judge had received a letter from a man called Henfield confessing to the job that Cleeve was done up for. Then he gives me the suicide bit again, says that's it and rings off.' Pypard paused again. 'But from the way he was telling it, sir, this Cleeve was well and truly topped.'

'That's right, sir,' Canning said eagerly. 'I remember that case, sir. Cleeve's was one of the last toppings before it went off the book. But he was done up all right.'

'So chummie seemed to think.' Pypard glanced modestly at his notes. 'Which would make it a queer old job, wouldn't it sir, if his dab turned up in the Judge's summerhouse?'

Gently said curtly: 'I'm not looking for a dead man.'

'No, of course, sir,' Pypard said. 'But it's strange the fuss this job is creating . . . like you, sir, coming down here from the Yard.'

Gently gave him a stare, and Pypard dropped his eyes.

'It was the same voice—you're sure of that?'

'Yes, sir, the same voice,' Pypard said. 'And coming from a phone box again. This time he talked a bit longer, and the accent got a bit thicker, like at first he was trying to keep it down. I reckon he could be an American.'

'An American!'

'That's how he struck me.'

'Would you know a South African accent if you heard one?'

Pypard looked doubtful. 'Not sure if I would, sir,' he said.

'Perhaps that's how he would sound over the phone, sir,' Canning suggested. 'I might have put Stoke down for an American. Or he could have been faking.'

But that had to be wishful thinking: nobody would put Stoke down as an American. But Cleeve . . . hadn't Gently himself suggested the probability of his taking refuge across the Atlantic?

The phone went. Pypard grabbed it; as he listened, his sallow face twisted in disgust.

'And that's all we need! The lady is here, sir. She's insisting on talking to you.'

Gently stared. 'Better let her in, then.'

'But sir, Stoke will be here any minute!' Canning objected.

'Shove Stoke into an interview room and see that he stays there until we are ready for him.'

Pypard was hanging on to the phone, his eyes worried. 'I've just had this rollicking from the C.C., sir. I have to live here after you've gone, and I don't want trouble with the lady.'

'It's me she's asking for.'

'All the same, sir, I've got a feeling that I'm sitting on a volcano.'

'Let her in.'

Very reluctantly, Pypard spoke to the phone.

'So you're not even a local man—just an outsider, sent down from London!'

This morning one had the impression that Angela Pewsey had taken a second wind.

The black dress had given place to a grey flannel two-piece and a lilac blouse with a ruffled front, to which was pinned a spray brooch set with turquoise and seed pearls. In her hand she carried a small embroidered bag and a pair of lilac gloves, and a fragrance of hyacinths came in with her to battle with the doggyness of Pypard's office.

Pypard, who had yielded his seat to Gently, had well-nigh bowed her into the room; and Canning, when he returned from giving instructions, remained standing awkwardly in a distant station.

'Please be seated, Mrs Pewsey.'

'I have been discussing your behaviour with the Chief Constable. There will be repercussions, you can be certain. Sir Timothy is considering a complaint to the Yard. It just isn't good enough for you to come down here, making yourself offensive to innocent people. In the first place you are a stranger, entirely ignorant of the situation, and in the second you are pursuing an utterly absurd line of enquiry. What amazes me is that, up till now, our own police have given you their support.'

'Thank you, Mrs Pewsey. But do sit down.'

'I have no intention of sitting down! It is not on my own account I have come here, though heaven knows I have reason. But luckily I understand the law, my own injuries I can remedy. I am here on behalf of someone who can't, a man who is being persecuted beyond belief.'

'You refer to Mr Stoke?'

'To the man my lying grandson set you to harass. And who, I understand, has been ordered to report here with identification, like a common criminal.'

'You have been in communication with him?'

'Indeed I have, and your allegations against him are ludicrous. His identity is in doubt with no one, as I am here to bear witness.'

She was quite magnificent, the *grande dame*, dressed and perfect in her part. Pypard was watching her with awe, and Canning standing practically to attention. The County, Sir Timothy, the Judge himself: all were riding on her elegant shoulders.

'Who do you say this man is, Mrs Pewsey?'

'I! I say he is a man known to me since earliest childhood. I played with him, went to school with him, was a close friend of his sister's.'

'And under what name did you then know him?'

'Under his own name, Jonathan Stoke, with a sister, Jennifer Stoke, and a father, Thomas Stoke. They lived near Prior's Compton, where I lived, and where you will certainly find record of them. So why have you ordered him to report here with his birth certificate in his hand?'

Gently hunched. 'And the person you knew then is the same man that you know today?'

'That's absurd, of course he is. How do you think I could be deceived?'

'After . . . how many years would it be?'

'What does that have to do with it?'

'For example, Mr Stoke was unwilling to have his fingerprints taken.'

Her eyes flamed at him. 'Yes—exactly! You wished him to

behave like a convicted criminal. How can his fingerprints prove anything?'

'They can prove who he is not.'

'But who is he supposed to be?'

'A man giving the identity of Jonathan Stoke.'

'Oh, what rubbish.' Her breathing was harsh. 'You want his fingerprints for another reason, don't you? You've decided to believe the lies Mark told you and you're trying to implicate Jonathan in the death of my husband. And it's just laughable, because his fingerprints can tell you nothing at all. Do you know why? It is because one day recently I showed him over the grounds, including the summerhouse. And that is why the poor man is so upset when you go bullying him for his fingerprints.'

Gently was silent.

'Don't you believe me?'

'Yesterday, you made no mention of this, Mrs Pewsey.'

'And why should I, tell me that? What are my private affairs to you?'

'Yesterday, Stoke was just a casual acquaintance. Today, you talk of taking him to the summerhouse.'

'Showing it to him, was what I said. In fact, we spent ten minutes there, admiring the view.'

'With your husband's knowledge?'

Her eyes sparked. 'If I said yes, could you disprove it? As it happened Arthur had gone into Bath, so I didn't tell him about it till afterwards.'

'But then you told him?'

'Why not?'

'And he offered no objection?'

'Why should he? He was aware that Jonathan was an old acquaintance, and was only sorry that he had missed meeting him.'

'What day did this happen, Mrs Pewsey?'

'Oh, please don't expect me to remember that. Since Friday my brain has been in a turmoil, and my ideas of time vague.'

It was neat, very neat; and a tale that might take a great deal of faulting. Yet at the same time, didn't she appreciate that the mere telling of it might be damning? All this while she'd remained haughtily standing, her eyes never swerving from Gently's, chin stubbornly advanced, the bag and gloves clasped in front of her. She was doing battle, battle for the pair of them: and that was the most damning thing of all.

'I understand that you claim to have a witness prepared to say he saw Jonathan at Erchildown on Friday. That is scarcely possible, since at the time in question he was talking to me on the phone.'

'He was talking on the phone?'

'Is that so surprising? He gave me a ring while he was in town. It was to confirm a lunch date for Saturday, when I was hoping to introduce him to Arthur.'

Gently gazed at her. 'And at what time was that?'

'At half-past two, or shortly after.'

'In effect, at the time when the Judge was shot?'

'That, of course, is for you to say.'

'I think that call was a remarkable coincidence.'

'Are you by any chance calling me a liar? The fact is that you never had a foot to stand on when you tried to drag Jonathan into his. The attitude of the police has been simple from the start. There never was any evidence that the shooting wasn't accidental. I suppose there may be a faint case for suicide, but even that would be purely conjectural.'

'You would . . . go along with suicide?'

'Yes. If I had to.'

'At first, you were opposed to that suggestion.'

'I am still opposed to it, but who can tell what is going on in another person's mind? Arthur was not a man given to brooding, but he had been called on at times to take disturbing decisions, matters involving life and death. I know his reputation for severity troubled him.'

'That he was known as a hanging judge?'

'Precisely. Some of his cases may have left their mark on him.'

Behind her back, Pypard was winking and making pretence of holding a phone. But in fact there had been slight change of nuance when the subject dealt with had become suicide. It was as though she had relaxed a little, felt that here there lurked no threat: instead, in the eyes that faced Gently, was a flicker of calculation.

'One of the cases you refer to was tried at Lewes Assizes.'

'Really?'

'The name of the defendant was Eric Trevor Cleeve.'

'Should I know that name?'

'Do you?'

'As a matter of fact, I do. Arthur mentioned it once or twice when he was in a reminiscing mood.'

'It was a case that troubled him?'

'I think perhaps it did. There was an outburst in court by Cleeve's brother. Arthur had to have him removed, and I believe he was subject to a fine.' Her eyes were mocking. 'Is it the suggestion that it was this case that was preying on Arthur's mind?'

'There has been question since of Cleeve's innocence.'

'That, of course, might have bothered Arthur.'

'It was your husband's summing up that decided the jury.'

'Then you may certainly have a point.'

'Would you care to confirm that?'

'As much as you like. I understand the inquest will be held on Thursday. If you are tired of Jonathan, I am quite prepared to give evidence of my husband's depressed state of mind.'

Was she playing him along, or did she seriously believe he might accept a deal like that? Now she was staring at him interestedly, as though watching to see which way he would jump. She had played her cards, stirred up the Chief Constable, shored up the weak points in Stoke's story, and now she was handing Gently an out: did it really seem so simple to her?

'Thank you, Mrs Pewsey.'

'You mean that's all?'

'Unless you have something else to tell me.'

At once her stare was quelling again and she clutched the bag and gloves more tightly.

'Oh no! If Jonathan has arrived, then I wish to be present at the interview. I asked Sir Timothy if I might, and he said you might well want to see us together.'

'I must ask you to leave, Mrs Pewsey.'

'And I say I will not, without Jonathan. You have persecuted the poor man unmercifully, and this time I intend to stand by him.'

'If necessary, I shall have you removed.'

'Then you will answer for it to the Chief Constable.'

'If you are wise, you will leave now without creating a breach of the peace.'

Her eyes blazed hate at him.

'Very well, then. But my first act will be to ring Sir Timothy. Because you come from London it doesn't mean that you can behave like a little Hitler. You have no case against Jonathan, nor any case at all, and I am astounded that our own police stand by and hear you threaten me with violence. Believe me, it will do them no good, and your own proceedings will be the subject of an official complaint.'

'Now you must go.'

'Don't think for one minute that you've heard the last of this little outrage.'

Canning hastily opened the door for her, and Mrs Pewsey stalked from the office. A few moments later they heard the slam of a car door and saw the green Lancia speed by down the street.

'Oh glory be!' Pypard groaned. 'I said I was sitting on a volcano. There's my promotion gone for sure, and I'll be lucky if it stops at that.'

'The lady was bluffing,' Gently shrugged.

'Then, for heaven's sake, don't call her bluff.'

'We have Stoke. She's scared that we'll break him.'

'Me, I'm beginning to be scared myself.'

'She was lying, sir,' Canning said. 'They've got together and cooked up a tale to get Stoke off. Only now we know where we can hit him. She's just about shoved him into our arms.'

'Yes,' Pypard said bitterly. 'With the Chief Constable watching us like a hawk. It was me who he just tore off a strip, and I can tell you he means business. What's wrong with a suicide verdict, anyway?'

'Not with that dab, sir,' Canning said.

'Didn't I hear the lady just explain it?'

For an instant, Canning looked worried.

Gently said: 'Check if Stoke has arrived, and if he has, wheel Hinton in here.'

'I give up,' Pypard said. 'In this one, there just aren't going to be any winners.'

Mrs Pewsey had brought in the scent of hyacinths; Hinton followed it with a pong of slurry: he had been hauled off a job in a cattle-byre, and his gumboots carried the evidence. He came in excitedly.

'You got him, m'dears. He's the one, no doubt about it. Didn't I tell you I'd know him again? Arr, and him knew me, too!'

'You recognised a man who came into the Police Station?'

'Right off I did, you ask this copper. Same car too, it's standing out there. Knew him as soon as he pulled up.'

'He was the man you saw on Friday driving past the entrance to the warren at Erchildown?'

'I'm telling you. And he knew me—didn't he glare just, as he went by me!'

Gently glanced at Canning's sergeant, who nodded. 'Stoke recognised Hinton, sir. He seemed concerned.'

'Concerned is right, m'dears,' Hinton chuckled. 'Him was carrying some packet, and him hid his face. So now who's a liar?'

'He was the man you saw in the car, and also the man you saw leave the summerhouse?'

'Yi, I'll swear to that. So now you've got him fair and square.'

'You will swear to it?'

'Isn't that what you want?'

'I want to know if you recognise him as the same man.'

'And I say yes—as well as one might, being as how I never saw that bloke close, like.'

'You would have seen him at a distance of three hundred yards.'

'Arr, well,' Hinton's rabbity mouth gaped. 'He was a tallish bloke, like this one. And I'd reckon the same age and all.'

'Did you see his face clearly?'

'Yi—I'd say. Only not so close to, was he?'

'But at the time you had no doubt that he was the same man who you saw later driving the car?'

'Well—no.' But Hinton's eyes were bothered. 'I never 'zactly thought there might be two of him, did I?'

'Tell me again about the one at the summerhouse.'

'So I shoves my head up, and I sees him. Coming out of there in a hurry, he was, and into the trees like a rabbit.'

'Into the trees on which side of the summerhouse?'

Hinton's eyes were yet more worried. 'The far side—towards the house.'

'Not the near side—towards the lane?'

'Well . . . I don't know.' He gulped. 'Suppose he was going like a deer, he might have got there. And he was out of that summerhouse sharpish, arr, and I can't be sure when I heard the car start.'

'Did the man driving the car seem breathless?'

'I can't say that—he turned his head, didn't he?'

'You saw his face first. Did his face look hot?'

Helplessly, Hinton shook his head.

'Does this suggest anyone?'

On Pypard's desk lay a copy of Heywood's photofit picture; Gently handed it to Hinton. Hinton gazed at it as though it might have been an object from outer space.

'But I still reckon him was only the one . . .'

And clearly, they weren't getting closer than that. Hinton was shown out, boots and all, leaving the rural pong behind him.

'So now for the big one, sir!'

Silently Gently lit his pipe. Out there at the summerhouse on

Friday, just what had happened in that spell of a few minutes? The picture wasn't clear. At the time of the shot there had certainly been two people in the vicinity, Hinton and Stoke, with the possibility of a third; while Mrs Pewsey herself could not be eliminated. It was the timing that had bothered Hinton, and it was the timing that bothered Gently. Things had happened too quickly! How many had been there, and what was their relationship with each other?

'Is the gun still here?'

'Yes, sir.'

'Wipe it carefully and stand it by the desk.'

Canning performed his task officiously and placed the gun beside Gently.

'Do you have a stenographer?'

'I'll see if she's in, sir.'

Canning fetched a dour-faced policewoman with a mole on her cheek. She was settled at a corner of the desk with her notebook, pencils and sharpener.

'Now we'll have chummie.'

The atmosphere in the office moved Pypard to open the window with a jerk; but the odour of Hinton lingered, along with the haze of Gently's pipe.

8

'Here are the documents you asked for. May I take it this line of enquiry is now closed?'

From the moment he walked in, it was apparent that Stoke had had some fire put in his belly. The evening before he'd been caught on the hop and then he had been shaky and defensive: not so now. He spoke with the tone of a man who felt he had a case to argue. If the presence of Hinton had disturbed him, he had had time to overcome that: time also perhaps to invent explanations, if explanations should become unavoidable.

'Take that chair, Mr Stoke.'

Stoke sat. This morning he looked a different man, too. In place of work clothes he wore a tailored tweed jacket with tan slacks and a suede waistcoat. Hang glasses on his shoulder, and he would cut the sort of figure one met at point-to-points or in race-track enclosures: a man very proper to escort Angela Pewsey and to go by her side in the green Lancia. Sitting, he spread his knees slightly and folded his hands before him.

'You have changed your mind about providing fingerprints?'

'No. I haven't changed my mind.'

'I may have some further questions to put to you.'

'Wouldn't you say that was a waste of time? There are my passport and birth certificate, and you can check them to kingdom come. Also you will find there the addresses of my relatives. What more can you want with me?'

'I shall need further information about your movements.'

'And I don't feel compelled to give it.'

'What you told me doesn't square with some other testimonies.'

'All you put to me last night I deny absolutely.'

So that was to be his line: sturdy denial, with Mrs Pewsey and the Chief Constable in his corner. Gently shrugged to himself and tipped out the contents of the folder Stoke had handed him. The birth certificate was a thirty-year-old copy of one issued at Prior's Compton in 1932, giving his father as Thomas Henry Stoke, farmer, his mother's name Elizabeth Mary. The passport had been issued two years earlier and bore the Peterborough stamp, had not been visaed and gave the impression of probably never having been used. The photograph showed Stoke with a deeper tan than now, but there was no question of the resemblance.

'You obtained this passport on returning to England?'

'I did. And the birth certificate when it says.'

Which meant that, if it was genuine, it supported his account of himself completely. Along with these items was a card on which he had written addresses in Cape Town and Pietermaritzburg, and an identity card and a driving licence, both issued in Salisbury, Rhodesia.

'Perhaps you are convinced now?'

'I accept that you are the owner of these documents.'

'Then I am free to go?'

'No.'

'Then if you must waste time, please ask your questions.'

Fixing his gaze on the other's eyes, Gently said: 'Let's begin with your movements on the Good Friday.'

Stoke's eyes flinched. His haggard cheeks darkened, and involuntarily he drew himself up straighter. He hesitated briefly, then snapped:

'That has nothing to do with your enquiry!'

'I think it has.'

'And I say it hasn't.'

'Do you know the name Mark Clevancy, Mr Stoke?'

'Yes I do, as it happens—'

'It was he who saw the cars parked at Wellbottom Tumulus. His relative's car he recognised, and in consequence went in search of her. He found her with you, and withdrew. But he took the number of your car.'

'Angela was in Bath, and I was in Salisbury.'

'Can you prove that statement, Mr Stoke?'

'I don't need to prove it. Young Clevancy is a liar, he would have every motive to tell such a tale.'

'He was able to give the number and description of your car.'

'He could have seen my car anywhere!'

'But why take the number?'

'How would I know? Simply to make mischief, it wouldn't surprise me.'

'But why your number?'

'Because he knew we were acquainted and that it would give some colour to his story.'

'But you had met again only three weeks previously, during which time Clevancy was at Cambridge. How would he know?'

'I can't tell you how he knew!' Stoke's composure was vanishing fast. 'Somehow he did. He may have seen us together here, then spied until he saw me go to my car. I don't know, and it doesn't matter. Even if it were true it is none of your business. There wasn't anything real between Angela and Pewsey, it was just a companionship marriage, that's all.'

'Your being her lover was justifiable.'

'I didn't say that. And it wouldn't matter.'

Gently shook his head. 'Yes, it matters. It matters because Clevancy tipped off Judge Pewsey, and because Judge Pewsey was in the process of making a new will, clearly not in favour of Angela Pewsey.'

'You can't know that. The draft was destroyed.'

'We know that it prejudiced Mrs Pewsey's interest.

'And from that you're trying to argue—'

'On the face of it, the Judge died at a time convenient to at least two people.'

'But that's insane!'

Gently stared. 'Now we'll come to your movements on the Friday of last week.'

'I won't answer any more questions.'

Some residual tan made the pallor in Stoke's face appear as a greyness. He was no longer sitting with clasped hands, but with doubled fists pressed to his thighs. Of the pair, Mrs Pewsey was the strong one: she would have hit back with an instant attack; it was easy to see why she had tried to be present. Stoke lied without conviction, he was the soft underbelly.

'Yesterday you gave me a rough timetable for your lunch on Friday at the Red Lion. Now that you've had time to think it over, perhaps you can make it more exact?'

'I won't answer, and you can't make me.'

'For example, weren't you seated by half-past twelve?'

'I won't discuss it!'

'According to the waitress, you were already at your table when the service commenced.'

'Then she is mistaken.'

'She remembers you reading a magazine through the meal.'

'That could have been anyone.'

'And that you left a fifty-pence tip, which she found when service ended, at two p.m.'

'I was there till later!'

'How much later?'

Gently nodded to the policewoman, who picked up a pencil. Stoke sent her a fearful look, holding himself tight and leaning a little forward.

'Why would I remember that exactly? Did I know I was going to be questioned? It was later than two, a good deal later, and I had some shopping to do after that. I picked up a filter, I told you about it.'

'Yesterday you placed that before lunch.'

'So now I've thought about it, and it was after.'

'The garage confirms your original statement.'

'Well—I don't know! Before or after, I had other shopping to do. Then there was the bank. I can only say for certain that I was back home by half-past three.'

'From two till half-past three your movements are uncertain?'

'No, it was just the way I said! I left the Red Lion say at

half-past two and did some shopping . . . and I made a phone call.'

'A phone call?'

'Is that unusual?'

'Would it have been made from the Red Lion?'

'I didn't say that. Actually, from a phone-box . . . the one beside the church.'

'Presumably an urgent call, since you would have been home shortly afterwards?'

'Well—no, not exactly urgent! But I happened to think of it, seeing the box.'

'And to whom did you make this call?'

'I don't see the need to tell you that.'

'Mrs Pewsey testifies that you rang her to confirm a lunch date for the following day. But such a call might have been made at any time on the Friday, so why from a phone-box—and at half-past two?'

'It just happened like that, that's all I can say!'

'Coincidentally, at half-past two?'

He nodded miserably.

'And if we can show that the phone-box by the church was out of order for the whole of that day?'

He hung on, eyes astare. 'You're bluffing!'

'That's for you to decide, Mr Stoke.'

'Oh God.'

His eyes panicked, darting away from Gently's gaze.

Gently said: 'You didn't make that call, because at that time you were seen twice in Erchildon, once leaving Judge Pewsey's summerhouse, once driving your car in the direction of Clyffe.'

'No. I have already denied that!' With an effort he made himself face Gently's eyes. 'I saw the fellow you had parked out there, and it isn't good enough, it won't stand up. You told him I was coming.'

Gently shook his head. 'His recognition was voluntary—as yours was of him.'

'I'd never seen him before!'

'Yet you hid your face.'

'I—I deny that. He was mistaken.'

'Haven't too many people been mistaken already?'

'I can't help it. He was lying.'

'He, Mark Clevancy, and how many others?'

'Oh my God.' He struck his knees.

Gently said: 'Let's start again. You left the Red Lion at some time before two. Then you drove to Erchildown and parked your car in the lane that leads to Erchildown Old Place. We'll take it from there.'

'But it wasn't like that!'

'It couldn't have been otherwise, Mr Stoke.'

'Yes it was—there's an explanation. But I didn't want to admit having been there, did I?'

Stoke looked in a mess. He'd begun sweating now, with drops starting to collect in the creases of his forehead, and his eyes were desperate, set in a scowl that focused somewhere just ahead of him.

Admittedly the atmosphere in the office was oppressive, with the odour of slurry still detectable. Occasionally the policewoman had given little sniffs, and once had glanced accusingly towards Stoke. But in his case, wasn't it fear she could smell?

Gently said: 'Just for the record! Up till now you have been lying to us?'

'Yes. No. Not lying. Only I didn't want to admit . . .'

'Between two and three o'clock you were at Erchildown.'

'It had nothing to do with what you're saying! A lot of people were at Erchildown . . . there was that fellow sitting out in the car.'

'But you were there?'

'All right. I was.'

'Parked in the lane near the Old Place.'

'Not parked—not like that. I pulled off there, that's all.'

'To meet someone.'

'Not to meet someone. I tell you, I can explain it if you'll only listen. I drove out there to make a call, but not . . . it wasn't Mrs Pewsey. It was about a muck-spreader.'

'About a what?'

He flicked at his sweat. 'A man out there had one for sale—it was advertised, I can show you the advertisement. I wanted one, so I went to look at it.'

'But you parked in the lane.'

'That was later, I tell you. I only pulled in there for a minute . . . just to, well, relieve myself. Something at lunch must have upset me.'

'And you drove to Erchildown just to look at a muck-spreader?'

'I can show you the advertisement if you don't believe me.'

'Ending up in the lane precisely when the Judge was shot?'

'I don't know that . . . I simply pulled in there.'

Gently shook his head almost in bemusement. So this was what Stoke had cooked up while he waited! That remembered advertisement must have seemed like an inspiration to provide deliverance in a tight corner . . .

'Then the owner of the muck-spreader can confirm your story. Perhaps you will oblige us with his name and address?'

'Yes, but he was out, I didn't see him. There was no one about the farm at all.'

'You didn't see him!'

Stoke flinched.

'Yet suppose we find that this man was at home?'

'I—I knocked, I tell you, but no one came. If he was there, I didn't see him.'

Was it even worth checking?

'Give me his name.'

'Yes . . . the Home Farm, the man's name is Kington. It's out of the village, down the Prior's Compton road . . . can I help it if he didn't see me?'

Gently nodded to Canning, who went out.

'Now let's suppose that someone is lying! The time is shortly after two o'clock, and you've just parked out of sight down the lane. What happens next?'

Stoke's lips were trembling and his face was blurred with sweat.

'I've told you what happened . . . I may have parked there ten minutes.'

'Longer.'

'At most ten minutes . . . I went up the lane, that's all.'

'You would have heard the shot.'

'No!'

'If what you say is true you must have done. You were seen to drive away within minutes of the shot being fired.'

'There's some mistake . . .'

'No mistake. You have admitted being there when the shot was fired. If a witness in the warren could have heard it, you must have heard it in the lane.'

'Then perhaps I did!'

Gently nodded. 'You heard it. Because you were closer to it than in the lane. The same witness who saw you drive away saw you a few minutes earlier, leaving the summerhouse.'

'I deny that! It's his word against mine.'

'Then why won't you let us take your fingerprints?'

'Because, because.' Anguishedly he dabbed at his eyes. 'There's a reason.'

'Then let's hear it.'

'It's true . . . I'd been in the summerhouse before.'

'You admit having been there?'

'Yes, but before! Not on the Friday . . . not then.'

'So when before?'

'Last week. Mrs Pewsey can tell you.'

'But I'm asking you.'

'One day last week . . . Monday, it may have been Tuesday.'

'Go on.'

'We met here in town. I wasn't busy . . . she offered to show me round the New Place. So we drove out there and walked round the grounds and she took me as far as the summerhouse.'

'She took you into the summerhouse.'

'She wanted to show me! There's a view from it of the White Horse.'

'She took you in, and you closed the door.'

'There was nothing like that at all. And I didn't close the door . . . we sat for a few minutes, just to see the view. Nothing else.'

'So where do your fingerprints come into it?'

'I was there. I could have left some.'

'Left them where?'

'How should I know! On a seat, somewhere . . .'

'Or somewhere.'

Reaching down, Gently hoisted Pewsey's gun by the trigger-guard. He slid it across the desk, the muzzle pointing at Stoke's midriff.

'What about this?'

Stoke's eyes were huge and his sodden face suddenly grey. He gazed at the gun as though at any moment he expected it to go off.

'You have seen it before, haven't you?'

'No, I swear. I've never seen it!'

'On Friday afternoon you had it in your hand. Only then it was pointing the other way.'

'I wasn't there!'

'Take it.'

'No!'

But Gently thrust the gun into his hands. Stoke grabbed it awkwardly by the barrel, holding it away from his body.

'Could you commit suicide with that gun?'

'Oh God, no!'

'Try it. Hold the muzzle to your chest, then reach for the trigger.'

Tremulously Stoke positioned the gun, but his shaking finger would reach only to the guard.

'Not suicide then, was it—even though we found the gun in his hand?'

'I won't . . . this is a trick!'

'So somebody was holding that gun on Friday.'

'It wasn't me.'

'You were seen at the summerhouse.'

'The fellow was lying. I never . . .'

'You were there. You were in the summerhouse.'

'I tell you no! I never touched . . .'

He slammed the gun back on the desk, knocking over Pypard's perpetual calendar. The policewoman jerked her pad aside, then went on scribbling down Stoke's last words.

'You have handled that gun before, Mr Stoke.'

'How could I?'

'Isn't that where your fingerprints may have been?'

He shuddered.

'That's why you wouldn't give them, and why you told this tale about an earlier visit to the summerhouse.'

'It's true, I'd been in the summerhouse before—'

'Yes—because it was a rendezvous for you and Mrs Pewsey!'

Stoke covered his face. Gently gestured to Pypard, who eagerly picked up the gun by the guard. Going out, he met Canning coming in. Canning shook his head: Stoke's muck-spreader alibi was bust, too.

'Now we will go over your movements again.'

A few minutes had passed since Pypard went out with the gun; in the interval Stoke had snatched back a degree of composure, even shakily wiping his gaunt face with a handkerchief. His eyes had a beaten look, but there was a defiance about him too. When he spoke his tone was bitter, the flat vowels even more evident.

'That business with the gun was a trick, wasn't it?'

Gently stared but didn't reply.

'Yes, a trick,' Stoke said huskily. 'To get my fingerprints. Like the fellow sitting in the car, another trick. You didn't have anything on me, really. I should have walked out of here straight away.'

Gently said: 'You didn't choose to co-operate. One way or another we would have had your dabs.'

'Why should I co-operate, when I wasn't guilty? Just making me hold the gun doesn't mean I fired it.'

'So let's go over your movements again.'

'No. I've said all that I'm going to say.'

'We know you didn't visit the Home Farm on Friday.'

Stoke shut his mouth tight.

'From the beginning you have told us lies.'

'But I didn't shoot Pewsey.'

'In that case you can tell us what you know. For example, at the summerhouse that afternoon, who else was there besides yourself?'

'Besides—?' His lips quivered. 'I tell you again, I wasn't there.'

Gently leaned closer. 'There really is no point in your lying any further! If you are innocent, as you claim, the sensible thing now is to help us. So who else was out there?'

Stoke's eyes were sick, and for a moment it seemed he might take the bait. But then a spasm went over his face, and he jerked:

'That fellow who was sitting outside in the car!'

'Then it was you. You alone.'

'And it's his word against mine that I was ever there.'

'We've been over all that.'

'It's still his word. And you've been saying yourself that I told you a tale.'

'So now let's have the truth.'

Breathing quickly, Stoke said: 'The truth is what I told you at first. I wasn't out there, I was shopping in town. And I rang Mrs Pewsey when I said.'

Gently's stare was marble. 'And you think I'll still believe that?'

'Why not? Since you haven't proved anything, yet.'

'Don't forget the gun.'

'I never touched it.'

'But you were right in supposing we found dabs at the scene.'

'Those—I explained about them.'

'Did you?'

Stoke tried to outface him, but couldn't. His little burst of defiance was leaking away, his eyes were desperate again, anxious. But if he stuck to the lie? Still it rested on the dab, that obstinate, improbable intrusion. If it were his, the case fell together, but if it wasn't . . . how much did he know?

'This is your chance. If you want to change your tale, it had better be now, in these next few minutes. After that it may be too late—and don't say you didn't have warning!'

Stoke croaked: 'I was in town. All the rest is a trick.'

'You handled that gun.'

'No.'

'Then you know who did.'

He trembled. 'I've finished. I'm saying no more.'

'You were at the scene. You saw what happened. The truth is your only way out. Either you tell it now, or you may find yourself sitting in a cell.'

'I've told it.'

'Till now, you've lied.'

'No. And I'm saying no more.'

'Don't think Mrs Pewsey's influence will save you.'

He groaned, but kept his mouth shut.

Canning said softly: 'It's good advice, sir. And you'll feel better when you've got it off your chest.'

Stoke stared at him with glazed eyes: he jammed his mouth tighter shut than before.

'Think it over, sir. You know we are right.'

But now Stoke wasn't listening. He was hugging his arms, staring at nothing, determined not to let slip another word.

Then Pypard opened the door. 'Sir . . . ?'

Gently rose and went out.

'Well?'

Pypard shook his head. 'Sorry sir, but after a quick check . . .'

The dab wasn't Stoke's.

'So what do we do now, sir?' Pypard's eyes were worried. 'If we charge him, we shall have the Chief Constable rolling up here in a tank. And you only got him as far as the lane, sir. We still can't place him closer than that.'

'He was there. He handled that gun.'

'But the dab is his out, sir. Like it was Hinton's.'

Yes, the dab was his out. And they hadn't broken him. And he had perhaps begun to realise that his lie might stand.

So, to hell with Stoke!

'Get him to write his statement, and try to make him tack on those admissions.'

'And then, sir?'

'Let him go. He wasn't your chummie on the phone, was he?'

'No, sir. Stoke sounds more like an Aussie. I'd say my man was a Yank for certain.'

A Yank for certain: and still out there somewhere, still hankering to drag in the memory of Cleeve, to make them understand that Cleeve was revenged. Because wasn't that why he was still haunting the district?

'Any results yet from that photofit picture?'

'Only one, sir. It's just come in. The Cross Keys at Erchildown think he might be a man who stopped there for lunch on Friday.'

'At Erchildown!'

'They couldn't swear to it, sir.'

Gently said: 'Stoke is all yours. Send Canning out here to me.'

'Yes, sir.'

Pypard looked relieved; though Stoke didn't know it, he had found a friend.

9

Gently's mood showed in his driving: a crispness just short of impatience. He was shrugging Stoke off, putting behind him the gaunt-faced colonial and his incompetent lies.

Chummie or no, Stoke wasn't his affair, had ceased to be so when the dabs failed to match: Gently's brief was the man who didn't hang, and the weight of the case standing against him.

And a cast-iron case it needs must be, to go forward without reference to motive: less than that, and Cleeve would be laughing. And already that case had been eroded.

But to hell with Stoke! Time now to forget him, a piece of routine cleared out of the way . . .

Canning said doubtfully: 'I'm still a bit confused, sir. I can't see how this other chummie fits in. Not unless Cleeve was the man who you say dodged the drop, and was still given out to have been topped.'

'Just go along with what I told you!' Gently grunted.

'Yes of course, sir. But it makes you wonder. Did they ever really top people in the old days, sir?'

'They topped them.'

'And Cleeve was topped, sir?'

'I've seen the doctor's post-mortem notes.'

'Then . . . if Cleeve is really dead, where does this other fellow come in?'

'He comes in as a dab left in the summerhouse. And probably as the man Hinton saw from the warren.'

'But then what has Cleeve to do with it, sir?'

'For the moment, nothing at all! We're after a chummie, one urgently needed. And perhaps we'll know more when we feel his collar.'

'Yes, sir. Urgently needed.'

Canning resumed a reluctant silence. But there was a gleam in his eye as they sped along the Prior's Compton road . . .

At the Cross Keys they were preparing for lunch and the two policemen were ushered into a spacious kitchen. There the landlord was sawing collops from a round of beef while his wife and the barmaid put up plates of salad. It was the barmaid who had served the man: she had placed him at once as a 'foreigner'. He had ordered a lager and a plate of chicken salad, and had taken them to one of the outside tables. And there was a bonus. Coming back for another drink, he had asked directions to the New Place.

'Did you see him leave?'

The barmaid nodded. 'He finished his drink in the bar. It was then he asked me about the New Place, and I saw him go off the way I'd told him.'

'In his car?'

'No, he left it parked here. He must have come back for it later.'

'Do you remember the time?'

'About two, I reckon. But I don't know what time he came back.'

'After three,' the landlord put in. 'There was only the one car left, and I heard it go.'

'Does anyone remember the car?'

The barmaid thought it might have been a Ford, but was uncertain about the colour. On the other hand, her description of the man's clothes tallied fairly closely with that given by Heywood. And as to accent:

'He spoke a bit quaint, like. Could have been an American, for all I know.'

It was slotting together. They had tracked Cleeve to Erchildown, and the times exactly fitted. If he had left the Cross Keys at two he could have been at the summerhouse by two-thirty or earlier. The Judge was shot at two-forty, Hinton had seen a man leave about ten minutes later; time then for Cleeve to reach his car at, say, three-fifteen and to turn up at the Red Lion a quarter of an hour later. But by what route had he reached the summerhouse . . . ? Clearly not by the main drive and the kitchen gardens!

'Let's see if we can pick up his tracks.'

'Yes sir. We might happen on something useful.'

Leaving the Rover parked at the Cross Keys, they set out over the green to rejoin the road. Within two hundred yards the road reached the fringe of the woods that ringed the New Place. The woods were fenced with hawthorn, fire-white against the shade of the trees, and groves of wild parsley reached waist-high along the verges. Old wire-netting supplemented the hawthorns, with fence-posts here and there sagging. At places, one could see through into the woods, which just here were azure with colonies of bluebells. Then they came to it.

'Look, sir . . . !'

Where Cleeve had entered was almost too obvious: the cow parsley was trampled, a fence-post collapsed and the rusty wire-netting trodden into a bag. The cow parsley was blackened and limp, bearing witness that the entry was several days old, and beyond it the bluebells were trampled in a direct line up the slope of the wood.

'Do we go in, sir?'

'First, we look.'

It was Canning who spotted their only find: on the other side of the gap, just short of the bluebells, a crumpled ball of blue paper and plastic. With care, they stepped over the wire-netting, and Canning retrieved the ball. It was a screwed-up cigarette pack, the paper a little damp.

'Chesterfields, sir—American fags.'

'It could have been tossed in from the road.'

'Not it, sir,' Canning averred. 'Because how many people round here smoke Chesterfields? I'd say it happened like this: after he broke in, he stood still for a minute, listening. Then, when he found it was all quiet, he lit up and chucked this packet away. Ten to one, when we grab him, we'll find a packet of Chesterfields on him.'

'So identify it and keep it safe.'

Canning took an envelope from his wallet. On it, he scribbled conscientiously before enclosing the crumpled packet.

'Shall we follow up, sir?'

'Stay clear of his tracks. And keep an eye open for soft ground.'

But the ground stayed unhelpfully firm as they worked their way up through the woods, accompanied by the sickly smell of the bluebells, which they couldn't avoid trampling on. Then the bluebells gave out, and so did the tracks, lost in an area of young bracken; they were left to extrapolate the line as well as they could towards the summit of the trees.

'He looks to have kept clear of the house, sir.'

'He would, if his rendezvous were the summerhouse.'

'So like that he knew which way to head, sir.'

Gently shrugged: it was certainly puzzling. Cleeve had arrived at Mazebridge on the Thursday, and his preoccupation with maps suggested that the district was strange to him. Even from the village he had had to ask direction, yet once in the wood his line was unhesitating. Was it a coincidence, or had someone drawn him a plan? Just what had passed between him and Pewsey?

'Spread out and see if we can pick him up again.'

They searched diligently through the bracken. Here the ground was rock-hard, while the fronds of the bracken were proof against bruising. Eventually it ended in a tract of undergrowth composed of bramble and snowberry, and there, in trampled rough grass, they came upon fresh traces.

'He's heading for the track from the house.'

If they were still following Cleeve, he had branched towards the left. Now he was traversing the slope of the woods, and one caught glimpses of the roofs below. At last they came out on the track at a point where it took a sharp bend in its ascent: below was a clear view of the house, above, the daylight at the top of the track. Could it be coincidence again that Cleeve had arrived at a position so well suited to observation—where he had virtually the whole track under survey, and concealment available from whichever direction? Had he been expecting Pewsey to come this way, and then been outmanoeuvred by the Judge?

'He'll have gone up the track from here, sir,' Canning opined. 'No need for him to take to the woods again.'

Gently was staring at an area of trodden grass behind an elder in the shoulder of the bend. An intended ambush? Standing there, invisible, Cleeve still had the track in view towards the house. But if it had been an ambush, it had been frustrated, and something . . . what? . . . had led Cleeve to the summerhouse.

'So let's keep following him.'

They continued up the track, where any traces of Cleeve had long been overlaid, and came out on the now-familiar scene of the summerhouse, warren and the view of the White Horse. Here cover ended, as the track led along the edge of the woods to the summerhouse: for a hundred yards Cleeve had been naked, either from below or to the waiting Pewsey. Perhaps he had come through the woods after all, to approach the summerhouse from the rear . . . ?

'I reckon chummie had an accomplice,' Canning said suddenly. 'I can't see how he worked it on his own, sir. If it was him who did it and not Stoke, someone had to lay it on for him.'

'That could be only one person.'

'Yes sir. And we know she was out of the house just then. I'd say she met chummie on the track down there, slipped him the gun and gave him his orders. Easy enough to get the Judge to the summerhouse, she just had to spruce him she was meeting Stoke there.'

'But Stoke actually went there.'

'Perhaps Stoke told the truth, sir, and if he was around it was just his bad luck. You must admit that your chummie is the more likely customer, him having been done for murder before.'

'Stoke handled that gun.'

'It may have been later, sir.'

'Not later. The timing is too tight.'

'So then perhaps they were all in it, sir, and Stoke was there to give chummie a hand.'

Gently shook his head. Cleeve wouldn't have needed a hand

to shoot a seventy-eight-year-old man, wouldn't have wanted one—straight in, straight out, a clean job with no witnesses. Could he have been wrong about Stoke's fear that his dabs were going to be found on the gun?

They reached the summerhouse, silent and innocent, with sun drowsing through its leaded panes. Behind it the overhanging trees were masked at the foot by dense growths of honeysuckle. And one way or another, Cleeve had arrived there, had entered and closed the door: either carrying the gun himself, or to find himself staring into its muzzle. Which? It scarcely mattered, for Pewsey. The end found him sprawling dead on the floor, while the murderer meticulously wiped the gun and closed the dead man's fingers round it. And then? Because ten minutes elapsed between the shot and Hinton's glimpse of the man leaving. Why had he waited, what had he done, before leaving that one dab when he opened the door? Pewsey hadn't been robbed or his body searched . . . but suddenly, a hiatus in the proceedings.

Grunting to himself, Gently prowled round the summerhouse, trying to surprise traces in the rabbit-cropped turf. To the rear, honeysuckle trailed over the roof and pressed close to the blank wooden walls. He parted it: there was space behind sufficient for a man to insert his body: and there below was trampled grass, while a tendril of the honeysuckle hung limp and wilted. Something else! In the wooden wall, at the height of five feet, an empty knot-hole: stooping to it, Gently found himself staring through at the door and a good part of the interior. Another ambush . . . and this time successful? But the hole was too small to have admitted the gun. Yet someone had stood there for a while, watching . . . watching for someone else to arrive.'

'See here.'

Canning took his place eagerly and applied his eye to the knot-hole.

'Well?'

'Chummie must have got here first, sir. He hid up and waited for Pewsey to come.'

'But why would he do that?'

Canning shrugged. 'Who knows, sir? Perhaps he was afraid that Pewsey might bolt. So he watches Pewsey safe inside before he comes round and lets him have it

It was credible, but the timing suggested that Pewsey would have got there first; and that added another difficulty to the reconstruction that Gently was striving to establish. At each end of the event, a problem of time! Cleeve had arrived too soon, and left too late. Well: perhaps there was a simple explanation that would make the time scheme fit.

'When chummie left he ran into the wood, so he was in a hurry then at all events.'

'He would want to get under cover quick, sir The shot could have attracted attention.'

But why wait ten minutes first?

'Let's see if we can spot the way he went.'

'Yes sir. I reckon he just cut across the angle, going back towards the track.'

Canning proved a true prophet. They found trampled nettles under the trees, and even the stabbed toe-marks of a runner, plain in a patch of leafy soil. But no doubt now about where Cleeve was heading: he was sprinting for the safety of his car. Just forty minutes later he had reappeared at the Red Lion, looking, Heywood had noticed, a trifle grubby They had his movements nailed down: when they laid hands on Cleeve, he would have some formidable questions to answer.

As they came to the track, Canning hesitated.

'Time for another talk with the lady, sir?'

Gently thought about it, then shook his head.

'We'll leave the lady to make her own running!'

Beside Gently's Rover on the Cross Keys' car park stood a silver-metallic Jaguar with a personalised number plate, and a dandified figure at one of the outside tables jumped up to greet them as they arrived.

'What ho! I felt you wouldn't be long, so I had them set up pints. How are crimes?'

It was Pagram, presiding over three mugs and a stack of sandwiches. Dressed in sharp tweeds with a yellow waistcoat, he looked completely out of place in that setting, as out of place as he looked at the Yard, where his fancy clothes were a byword. But a keener mind there didn't come. Gently dropped on a chair and swigged beer.

'Any progress at your end?'

'Lots, old man. I thought I'd run down and talk to you in person. All about a visiting professional man, who was staying till lately at the Park Lane hotel.'

'A professional man?'

'Quite a good one, I'm told.' Pagram glanced at Canning. 'But your news first. At Mazebridge I heard you'd nabbed one hot prospect, and were hard on the trail of another. Would that be our playmate?'

Gently nodded. 'He arrived in Mazebridge at tea-time on Thursday.'

'Roger. My professional man booked out of the Park Lane on Thursday morning.'

'He lunched here on Friday, then set out on foot. We've tracked him through the woods to Pewsey's summerhouse. Pewsey's wife may have supplied the gun, and he was seen leaving the summerhouse after the shooting. The times match.'

'Oh dear.' Pagram made a comical face. 'That bit about Pewsey's wife is unfortunate. I can see the Sunday papers now. Are you sure she is strictly necessary?'

Gently shrugged. 'If it's to be a case, we may need her.'

'And is it a case?'

'You've heard what we've got.'

'Oh dear. And alas. And goddamn.' Pagram swigged beer. 'What about this Stoke fellow?'

'He's the reason why we need every shot in our locker.'

'And that poacher—he's a dead duck?'

'Hinton will be the chief prosecution witness.'

'Yuk.' Pagram swigged more beer. 'This really is a naughty

business. Certain persons are asking certain other persons why Barnes wasn't put down years ago. Panic is stalking the Corridors of Power. Their only hope is that it will all go away. And now you come up with a lurid case, a lover, Lady Macbeth and the trimmings. Old man, you won't be popular. I should vote Labour at the next election.'

Gently took a sandwich. 'So what about your end?'

'That's girl's talk.' Pagram grinned at Canning. 'Sorry, old lad, but the maestro and I will need to have words on our own.'

'Yes sir,' Canning stammered. 'I'll leave, sir.'

'No hurry. Drink your beer.'

In the end, after beer and sandwiches, they went to sit in Pagram's car. There the dapper Yard man unbuckled a briefcase and handed a telephoto print to Gently.

'That's him, hot from Ottawa. Neil Macready, insurance executive. Age 47, wife and three children, runs a branch of Great Lakes Assurance in Hamilton, Ontario.'

'Hamilton . . . ?'

'Did I hear a click?'

'It was the name he booked under at Mazebridge.'

'So there,' Pagram said. 'No deception. My man is yours, and tickety-boo.'

Gently stared long at the telephoto print, which showed Cleeve smiling, and was probably a press picture. Heywood's recall had been good, but here the smooth photofit image was supplemented by detail and the breath of life. The features were thicker, more lined, gave the impression of good living, and the carefully-styled hair was greyer than Heywood had remembered. Unchanged from the records photographs were the large, sensitive eyes, only now without their haunted look. It was the image of a successful man.

'How did you get on to him?'

'Oh, genius on my part.' Pagram buffed his nails complacently. 'I got on to a certain Mrs Grimsdyke, housekeeper to the late governor of Crampton. Mathieson had a brother, Alexander Mathieson, by rich coincidence also in insurance, also an employee of Great Lakes Assurance and at that time their general manager in Montreal. Mrs Grimsdyke knew him well. He often came over on visits to his brother. He was on a visit here at the critical date and departed on the very day of the alleged execution.'

'On a flight to Montreal?'

'On a flight to Montreal, which was where I next applied for illumination. It appears that at about this time there turned up in Montreal an English-educated nephew of the said Alexander. Canadian, of course, with a Canadian name as common as Smith or Jones over here, but English of accent, and purely by chance an insurance claims clerk by occupation. Alexander, that kindly man, took him on, and he rose through the ranks of Great Lakes Assurance. Now he manages the branch at Hamilton, a city about the size of Bristol.'

'Neil Macready.'

'Would I deceive you?'

'With at the moment an excuse for being in England.'

'Only the best. He was Great Lakes' delegate at an international underwriters' conference last week. It ended on Wednesday, but Mr Macready expressed the intention of staying on to see a little bit of Britain. He's driving a fawn Cortina, did you know that? It's rented from Godfrey Davis until Friday.'

'Have you the registration?'

'Naturally. Though he may have dumped the car by now.'

'He was still around here earlier today.'

'Alas, you're going to nab him. I can see that.'

But would they? So far, since the killing, Cleeve had stayed a wandering voice, though the photographs and the photofit picture had been circulating throughout the district. He was playing it clever, probably had dumped the car, certainly wouldn't return it to the agents; and while they might set a watch at the airports, mightn't he be shrewd enough to evade it? One weakness only Cleeve had shown: he had wanted them to know that he was avenged.

'Did you advise Ottawa of his true identity?'

'I told them a teeny fib, old man. I said we suspected

Macready was a certain Eric Cleeve who Inland Revenue desired a word with.'

'Are they checking on him?'

'Probably making notions, but Macreadys abound from coast to coast. Unless they get their hands on his Macready birth certificate I can't see them running him down. But that's academic. Both Mathiesons are dead, and we certainly won't prosecute the surviving conspirators. Your case, my lad, is against Macready, and nothing else but that will do.'

Gently said: 'If Cleeve plotted to kill Pewsey, then it was he who took the gun to the rendezvous. Which means quite certainly that there was a conspiracy between Cleeve and Mrs Pewsey. She had motive. Pewsey knew about Stoke and was drafting a new will. Only she could have provided the gun and had an opportunity to do so.'

Pagram looked solemn. 'Is that established?'

'At the critical time she was seen returning from the direction of the track to the summerhouse. We have traced Cleeve's route through the woods to the summerhouse and found indications of his having waited by the track. It had to be then, after Pewsey had left, because otherwise Pewsey might have missed the gun.'

'Nasty,' Pagram said. 'Very nasty. I can see the journalists busting a gut. But I can also see the Public Prosecutor asking for evidence of such a conspiracy. Do we have it?'

'Not yet.'

'Praise be for small mercies,' Pagram said. 'Is the lady a good liar?'

'None better.'

'I really would,' Pagram said, 'give the matter some thought.'

Gently hunched—no need to tell him! In the case against Cleeve it stood out bleakly. Some evidence there would have to be shown of his previous contact with Mrs Pewsey. On the face of it nothing could seem less likely than an acquaintance between her and the man from Hamilton, plus the knowledge of his secret—to what more improbable person could he have revealed it?

'Do we know if Cleeve had connections in Wiltshire?'

Pagram shook his head. 'Forget it, old man. He came from near Canterbury, born and schooled there. I've been checking back to locate the brother.'

'And did you?'

'The brother works for Shell, is innocently engaged in Abu Dhabi. Nothing there. You'll have to do better before you can unleash your Lady Macbeth.'

'The rest fits together.'

'Oh quite. But leave out the lady supplying the gun.'

'In that case Pewsey had it, and Cleeve took it off him.'

'Yes,' Pagram said. 'Keep it in. I like it.'

Gently stared out at the sunny green, where children played and women stood gossiping. How often, in the past, had he and Pagram discussed cases, with the latter playing the role of devil's advocate! A contemporary at the Yard, Pagram was now his superior, Gently having refused the step to Commander; it made no difference. They could read each other's thoughts, often conversing in a sort of shorthand. Almost always something new, a fresh viewpoint perhaps, would come out of their discussions.

'Punctures,' Pagram said, also staring at the green. 'Do tell me some more about this Stoke. The Pypard man was on pins, quite certain you would jump in with a charge.'

'There's a case, but Cleeve's dab wrecks it.'

'Forget the dab. Was Stoke at the scene?'

'He was seen there. He admitted being there. And he was scared to let us have his dabs.'

'Nice,' Pagram said. 'And I take your point earlier. It confuses the case against Cleeve. And Cleeve confuses the case against Stoke. Just thinking, but can't you link those two together?'

Gently thought about it. Two things stood out: Stoke's fear, and the minutes lost by Cleeve after the shooting. In some way, could they be connected, perhaps in some exchange between the two men? Suppose Stoke had heard the shot, had gone to investigate, rushed into the summerhouse moments after the shooting . . . and at some stage had handled the gun, while Cleeve plunged into explanations? Assuredly Stoke, after his first alarm, would see no inconvenience in the death of the Judge, would need little persuasion to make him keep his mouth shut and become an accomplice after the fact. So he would have left Cleeve to tidy up and have hastened back to his car, to be seen driving away by Hinton minutes after Hinton saw Cleeve leave the summerhouse. A credible scenario?

Grudgingly, Gently admitted: 'It's just possible.'

'Work on it, old son,' Pagram urged. 'It will go down much better with the lady left a grieving widow.'

'If Stoke knows about Cleeve he may spill it.'

'Any risk of that, and you walk away.'

'But suppose I'm left holding a detailed confession?'

'Upstairs,' Pagram said. 'Straight upstairs.' He glanced at his watch. 'Now I must go and make my report to our masters. Bung-ho, old top, and rather you than me holding the sharp end.'

Gently climbed out of the Jaguar, and Pagram gunned his engine and slid away. Once more, he had given a case a nudge, found for it a different perspective. Cleeve and Stoke . . . yet why had Stoke been there, at that critical time and place? Had Cleeve, by pure chance, interrupted another and quite separate conspiracy?

The Jaguar had barely vanished when two other cars entered the village, the first Mrs Pewsey's green Lancia, driving with dash towards the New Place. Beside her sat Stoke—so she had sprung him!—a drooping figure beside the upright driver; they saw Gently, and Mrs Pewsey glared at him as she swept by. The second car was a police Granada containing Pypard and two plainclothes men. It hauled up with a squeak of tyres and Pypard ran down his window.

'Sir—we're on to him!'

'On to who?'

'Your chummie, sir. He's at Prior's Compton. We had a tinkle from the Beauchamp Arms, and they're pretty certain he's the bloke. Accent, right clothes, driving a rented fawn

Cortina. He's out somewhere at the moment, but we aim to collar him when he comes in.'

The moment of truth?

'On your way, then!'

Canning was hastening over from his table. The Granada shot away towards Prior's Compton, and, a moment later, the Rover followed.

10

Prior's Compton was a large, stone-built village through which ran a broad, level street, set in a basin of the downs, with its own view of the brooding White Horse. Some of Mazebridge's insouciance seemed to linger about its sunny houses, whose warm stone contrasted with the fresh green of a row of limes. There must have been a stable in the vicinity, since riders walked their horses under the trees, while old men with pipes sat watching the scene from benches in the shade. There was little traffic. A few cars were parked in an open space by public toilets. Then a few more behind a dwarf wall that enclosed parking before the Beauchamp Arms. Here, beside the pavement, a police Escort waited, with a uniform-man standing beside it; Granada and Rover pulled in, and Pypard jumped out.

'Any sign of him?'

'Not yet, sir.'

'Nor there won't be with you parked there! Isn't there somewhere out of sight?'

'Yes sir . . . but I thought I'd better stay with it.'

In the end the Escort and Granada were driven to concealment behind the hotel. Gently parked the Rover, which was unmarked, immediately inside the forecourt. The keys he handed to one of the plainclothes men.

'If chummie drives in here, block the entrance.'

'Yes sir . . . a fawn Cortina.'

'Memorise this registration number.'

Pypard said: 'Then we know the car, sir?'

'Also, we have this recent picture.'

They clustered round to stare at it, four pairs of hard eyes. Then Pypard said, casually:

'Perhaps now we know his name too, sir?'

'Neil Macready will be the name on his passport.'

'He's booked in here as Wentworth, sir.'

Hamilton was in Wentworth County, Ontario.

They went into the hotel, where the manager fielded them at the door. A plump, bearded man with a gold tooth, he seemed more concerned even than Heywood had been.

'If I'd seen the pictures yesterday myself . . . as it happened I had gone into town to bank. I don't want you to think . . . Mr Pypard can tell you! Here, we always do our best to assist the police.'

'How long has the man been here?'

'Since Friday. I mean, if I'd had the least suspicion! But we often have Americans staying here, and he was the better sort of American. At once, as soon as I saw the picture . . .'

'At what time on Friday did he arrive?'

'At half-past four, I can tell you precisely because we were in the middle of serving tea.'

The manager's name was Fittleton, and he too had noticed that on Friday Cleeve had had grimy hands, also that he had been perspiring and seemed in a hurry to get through the formalities. In the register appeared the same neat handwriting as that in the register of the Red Lion: 'A.B. Wentworth', followed by the same non-committal address: 'London'. Having signed in, Cleeve had gone to his room and stayed there until dinner.

'How has he spent his time since he came here?'

'Well, I can't tell you. Mostly he's been out. But that's usual, people want to see the country, visit Bath, Stonehenge, Salisbury. How was I to know?'

'There's a coin-operated call box in the hall. Did he ever use it?'

'Yes, this morning before he went out. He came to the desk for change.'

'At what time was that?'

'Soon after nine. He isn't . . . I mean . . . he couldn't be Mafia?'

'Give me his keys.'

For Fittleton, all this probably couldn't have happened at a worse time; lunch was still in progress, the bar was open and customers were circulating in the hall. With a uniform-man in attendance, the little group at the desk at once drew attention. People loitered on their occasions, or returned to stare from doorways.

'You had better make yourself scarce, constable.'

'Yes sir . . . perhaps the office?'

He was given a chair from which only his face was visible as he peered, through a glass panel, towards the door. Then the flustered Fittleton led the way upstairs, avoiding the eyes of guests coming down, and took them quickly to a door at the end of a short passage.

'Is there likely to be trouble? I mean . . .'

'We don't want trouble any more than you.'

'But if he's armed . . . in a place like this . . .'

'We have no reason to suppose him armed.'

'Oh lord, why did he come here, of all the places he might have picked! Even here, in Prior's Compton . . .'

Gently eased him aside and unlocked the door.

The room was smallish, rather bleak, and equipped with the sort of furniture one found only in hotel bedrooms, a low divan bed, varnished wardrobe and dressing-table, a washbasin with a shelf and two low-seated chairs. Some toilet gear lay on the shelf and on the dressing-table a brush and comb, then there was a fancy imitation crocodile-skin suitcase laid flat on one of the chairs. The bed had been made.

'Since the customer went out, would this room have been serviced?'

'Certainly. Every morning—'

'Tell me what the maid does.'

'Well, she makes the bed, doesn't she, and empties the ashtray and bin . . . then she dusts, and wipes the washbasin, and finishes up hoovering the carpet.'

'Would she have wiped the toilet shelf?'

'Yes, she should have done.'

At last Gently entered the room. Still he touched nothing until he came to the suitcase, then with one finger he tipped back the lid. Cleeve hadn't unpacked. The capacious case was still stuffed with shirts and underwear, while even a suit in a plastic envelope hadn't been put away in the wardrobe. Gently opened it to reveal the label: Ridley Tailors, 115 Niagara Ave. On the shirts, other labels suggested a transatlantic origin. Gently felt in the elasticated pockets and his fingers touched something flat and square: Cleeve's passport! He withdrew it carefully, by a corner.

'Here.'

Pypard ventured in, and they examined the passport together. It had been issued in Ottawa to a certain Neil Henry Macready. National status: Canadian Citizen. Place of birth, Montreal. Date of birth: 3 Feb 35. Height: 1.82m. And a photograph that was almost a facsimile of that provided by the Canadian police.

Pypard whistled through his teeth. 'No doubt about him, sir. And he's the chummie who left the dab?'

'If he isn't you'll be left holding Stoke. So let's see if we can raise a latent.'

Pypard had brought the gear with him and now he and the detective-constable went to work. At first it seemed that Murphy's law was operating and that final proof must wait for Cleeve. They drew a blank on the passport, the shiny suitcase, the toilet shelf and gear, while the door offered only stranger prints, doubtless those of the maid. But at last persistence paid off. The glass top of the dressing-table yielded nothing, but when they began on the drawers Pypard gave an excited yip.

'There's one here, sir—his for a dollar!'

They clustered round while he made a comparison. On the front of the drawer, a clear thumb-print, identical with that on Cleeve's record card.

'Now see what's in the drawer.'

Canning eased it open, and honest joy showed in his face. The drawer contained an opened 200-pack of Chesterfields, from which two individual packs had been removed.

'We've got him now, sir. We've got him cold!'

Quite suddenly, Gently's chummie had become their chummie: still a man of mystery, perhaps, but a flesh-and-blood chummie, up for grabs. Pypard, especially, was hugging himself, with the spectre of having to charge Stoke receding—Stoke they couldn't get closer than the Old Place lane, while this chummie was nailed down to the spot. All they had to do now was catch him, and a trap was set for his innocence. His car was known, his base invested, in maybe minutes he'd walk into their hands . . .

But would they be feeling quite so euphoric if they knew the true picture of the man called Macready?

Gently turned to the unhappy Fittleton, who was still lurking in the passage:

'You must know this man's habits. At what time does he usually come in?'

'Really, I can't be held responsible! Twice, I know he has turned up for tea.'

'He parks his car out front?'

'Yes, of course. Only the tradesmen use the back.'

'We'll get him all right, sir,' Pypard said. 'I'll have Easton cover the back. Then there's Ashley watching the front. As soon as he comes through that door, we'll have him.'

'Oh dear,' Fittleton moaned. 'People may get hurt . . .'

'Don't you worry, sir,' Pypard said. 'You'll never know there's been a pinch.'

They went down again, with Pypard revelling in his arrangements. By now lunch was over and two waitresses were clearing the tables. The bar had closed, a certain somnolence was settling over the Beauchamp Arms; soon there was only the bartender left, rinsing glasses and whistling to himself. How long to wait? It was nearing three, and tea was served from four till five. And Cleeve . . . would he walk in quite so blithely, knowing as he must that he had tipped his hand? The two phone calls had each shown guilty knowledge, and he must be aware that the police were seeking him. So wouldn't he be on the watch for just such straws as a man waiting outside in a car?

'Let's split up between the dining-room and lounge.'

Each had windows overlooking the street. Pypard took the former, Gently the latter, Canning tagging along with him. The street, too, seemed in a siesta. You could count the pedestrians on one hand. In the Rover the detective-constable slumped sulkily, looking as though at the point of drowsing off. Gently lit his pipe and settled down to watch. After a while, Canning lit up too. Then for a space time passed leadenly, with even the bartender's whistle mute.

'Sir . . . he could have spotted us coming in.'

Gently bit on the stem of his pipe.

'If he did, what do you reckon he would do?'

'Just for now, keep your mind on the job!'

But the point was valid; they had taken no special precautions when they arrived, while the local constable and his Escort might already have been posted there for an hour. Had Cleeve seen it, and drawn his conclusions? They had found no money left in his room. In possession of his cash, even without the passport, he might very well find ways to give them the slip. Against this his routine heretofore had been to absent himself from breakfast until the tea hour . . .

At last the Prior's Compton vacancy was broken by the arrival of three of the horse-riders. A man and two ladies, they rode into the forecourt and hitched their nags to a rail provided. Time, three-fifty; they were breaking for tea. One heard them talking gaily as they passed down the hall, no doubt on their way to the washrooms for a tidy-up before seeking the lounge. And then:

'Sir—look!'

On the other side of the wide street, driven ever so slowly, a fawn Cortina: with the shaded face of the driver turned towards the Beauchamp Arms.

'It's him, sir. It has to be.'

But the row of limes was between them and the car. As it drifted by, at walking pace, no clear view of the number plate was possible. Pypard came hustling in.

'Did you see him?'

'We saw a fawn Cortina pass.'

'It's chummie—and he's sussed us! That's why he was driving past like that. Sir, let's get after him.'

'Wait. He can't get far now we know the car.'

'But if he dumps it—'

'Look, sir!' Canning exclaimed. 'He's turned, and now he's coming back.'

Still on the other lane in the street, the Cortina gentled past again, its driver's eyes fixed on the hotel, the windows, the horses, the man sitting in the Rover outside. Had he really sussed them, or was he just being cautious, reassuring himself that all was well? Once more the car passed on and continued out of sight.

'Sir, I'm going after him!' Pypard jerked. 'You can see he isn't going to risk it. Something must have tipped him off—maybe it was Ashley, in the car.'

'The car may be bothering him, but hang on.'

'I don't think he's coming back.'

'He knows he has to expect attention, so he's playing it canny. Give him his head.'

'This time he's away—'

'No—here he comes, sir!' Canning had his face pressed to the window. 'And this time he's on our side.'

'Get back from that window!' Gently snapped.

Now they could see the car's registration, and the face of the driver too. As he came in, his eye was on the Rover and on the apparently half-asleep man lolling in it. A tense face, the eyes wary, mouth pressed in a drooping line: he tickered the Cortina in softly, and softly reversed it to park facing the entrance.

Then everything happened!

First, the Rover's engine roared and it bucketed forward to block the entrance. Almost simultaneously there was a second roar, and the Ford leaped off on a collision course. For an instant Gently's precious Rover seemed about to become a write-off, but then the wheel of the Ford was twisted and it struck a stone wall with an almighty crash.

'Come on—get him!'

They raced out of the lounge, nearly bowling over a horrified Fittleton, and arrived in the forecourt just in time to see the detective-constable sent staggering by a hearty clout to the jaw.

'Grab him—grab him!'

Easier said than done! Cleeve made a sudden dart towards the whinnying horses, grabbed the rein of a big hunter and vaulted expertly into the saddle. Canning hurled himself at the horse: Cleeve met him with a foot in the chest. The next moment Cleeve had sailed over the dwarf wall and was clattering away down the street.

'Oh lord!' Pypard gaped. 'If he gets on the downs we'll have a real jamboree on our hands. For Christ's sake, let's get after him!'

And the four of them piled into Gently's car.

Cleeve was heading towards Mazebridge and he was a quarter of a mile up when they sighted him, an energetic figure crouched over his nag like a jockey down the finishing straight. Here the road was flanked by orchards in bloom and by dense hedges of hawthorn, but not far ahead, Gently remembered, there was access in plenty to the rolling downs. Soon they would be up with him, but how did one corral a horse and a determined rider? Halting a car was a familiar routine, but the text-books said nothing about a horse. . . .

'Can I use your radio, sir?' Pypard asked.

'What we need is a detachment of cavalry!'

'If we block the road ahead, sir, we might corner him.'

'By then he'll be over a hedge and away.'

Nevertheless, Pypard called in and alerted a patrol heading south from Erchildown. Then he got on to one at Clyffe with orders to converge from the flank. Meanwhile they were closing up fast on the flying hooves ahead: the moment had arrived to try something, however unlikely it was to succeed.

'Drop your window and try talking to him.'

Gently accelerated till they were level. Pypard ran down his window and above the confusion of slipstream, engine and hooves, bawled:

'Macready . . . you're under arrest!'

The result of that was that Cleeve reined in suddenly, so that the Rover shot ahead. Gently stood on his brakes. They squealed to a halt, a hundred yards ahead of the now stationary horseman. Gently jumped out and ran towards him. At once Cleeve began to back off. Gently stopped. Cleeve stopped. The others hustled up; Gently waved them back.

'The game is over, Macready—you may as well stop wasting everyone's time.'

'If this is a hold-up, forget it, buster. I can take care of myself, too.'

'Macready, you know us for policemen. I'm asking you now to give yourself up.'

'And I'm not falling for it, buster. Just fade away, and let honest folk be.'

Could he credibly believe they were bandits? Whether or no the result was the same: they weren't getting near him: a step forward by Gently was followed immediately by steps backward by Cleeve.

'Stay back, fellers!'

'You're being foolish, Macready.'

'Then I'll be foolish sitting right here.'

'You can't get away, so why keep it up?'

'If you want me, you catch me—yippee!'

He dug heels into the horse, which reared and whinnied, then turned it and began trotting back towards the village. One thing was plain: he was an expert horseman. He looked depressingly at home in a saddle.

'Back to the car.'

They piled in again, and Gently backed the car into an orchard entry; but just as he was going for forward gear he felt Pypard's hand tighten on his arm.

'Holy Moses—look at this!'

Cleeve had turned again and was galloping towards them

along the verge. As he came he waved a hand high, as though he might have been waving a Stetson.

'He's going to jump us!'

It seemed past doubt: the horse came on with unslackened speed. Involuntarily they ducked, but a few yards from them the horse baulked with a neighing and scuffling of hooves. Cleeve nearly went; the horse's legs were splaying, and he was hanging on by the neck. Then both horse and rider recovered, and Cleeve cantered away with a whoop of triumph.

'He'll destroy that bloody hack!'

The affair was beginning to turn into farce. Stone-faced, Gently swung the car again and set off after the vanishing horseman. And if he made the downs? Then they'd probably need the army if they were to flush him out of that . . . in all the information dug up by Pagram, why no mention of the fact that Cleeve was a horseman?

For a second time they overhauled him, to be greeted by a wave and a 'Yippee!'—but now Gently slotted in behind and contented himself with tracking the rider. The horse, a roan, was sweating heavily, and Cleeve had dropped his canter to a trot. That bad landing had doubtless shaken it, and certainly the horse should be tiring. But the downs were getting closer. Pypard stared after the horseman with fiery eyes.

'We're going to lose that bastard, sir. There's a lane up here within quarter of a mile. It leads to a farmer's barn, and then straight out into the downs.'

'What do you suggest? Could we block it?'

Pypard hissed. 'I doubt it, sir.'

'So?'

Pypard shrugged, and they went on following the horse.

The lane arrived: Cleeve turned down it; Gently wheeled the Rover in after him. Here they were bumping over a rutted surface where hawthorns almost met overhead. Now Cleeve dropped the pace to a walk, but there was no possibility of their overtaking him; insolently, he swaggered along ahead, with the Rover bumping behind in second. They passed the barn, turned a bend, saw the green swell of downs lifting before them

. . . but something else too: at the end of the lane, a very solid-looking five-barred gate.

'Oh jiminy!' Pypard groaned. 'We might have had him if the so-and-so had been driving a car. Here he goes, sir. This is the last we'll see of him for a few hours.'

Unhesitatingly Cleeve clapped heels to the roan, and the roan sprang forward into a gallop. Gently jammed on the accelerator and the groaning Rover went bouncing in pursuit. Hard at the gate went the sweating horse and crouched to make its spring: Gently hit his horn: the horse faltered in its rise and came down in a bundle on the far side of the gate.

'Now!'

They poured out of the car, and Canning demonstrated his agility by vaulting the gate. Cleeve had sprung up unharmed from his tumble and was racing away towards the green hills. Canning sprinted after him like a hare, with the detective-constable on his heels. Then came Pypard, bawling, and at a more sedate pace, Gently. Canning won. His tackle wasn't a model, but it brought Cleeve stumbling to the turf. Still he struggled, till the detective-constable came down on him with a thump.

'You tricky bastard!' Pypard panted, rushing up. 'So you can ride a horse, can you?'

'Lay off, you roughnecks!' Cleeve gasped. 'All I've done is borrow a nag.'

'All he's done, the man says!'

'Listen, I'll write the guy a cheque—'

'Not you,' Pypard panted. 'You won't write cheques. Not where you're going, sonny boy.'

'Let him get up,' Gently said.

Canning and the D.C. unravelled themselves. Cleeve, dishevelled and grass-stained, his greyed hair awry, got shakily to his feet. Gently stared into the smudged face, at the fleshy cheeks, beginning to pouch, the pallid mouth, beginning to droop, and the unchanged, warm brown eyes. So this was he: the unhung man, who had marched with pinioned wrists to the drop! And who, out of that nightmare, had conjured a new life, a new identity, a successful career. What could have prompted him to stake it on a throw that might lead him once more to the dock?

'Eric Trevor Cleeve?'

The brown eyes stared back at him without a tremor.

'My name is Chief Superintendent Gently and I am investigating the death of Judge Pewsey. My inquiries lead me to believe that you can help my investigation.'

'Right—but what was that name again?'

Gently said: 'Eric Trevor Cleeve.'

Still the eyes held. 'I've never heard of the guy. I'm Neil Macready, of Hamilton, Ontario.'

'Heard of him!' Pypard snarled. 'You've heard of him. This morning you talked about him to me on the phone.'

'That's crazy.'

'You're him, and you know it.'

'I'm Neil Macready. Just try to prove different.'

Nervously he dug in his pocket to pull out a crumpled pack of cigarettes. Canning had won his bet: they'd grabbed chummie with the Chesterfields on him.

The Cortina, though bent, was still driveable, and they stowed Cleeve's belongings in the boot. The horse had been caught by the detective-constable, who had ridden it back gingerly to its outraged owner. Fittleton's concern was for his bill, which he had hurriedly prepared and presented to Pypard.

'If you don't pay it, who will?'

To cut him short, Pypard had accepted it.

Then they set off back to Mazebridge, Rover, Granada and battered Cortina, with Cleeve travelling in the Granada and Pypard accompanying Gently. As they passed the lane Pypard gazed at it ruminatively, and at the White Horse on the slopes beyond. He sent Gently a cautious glance.

'A queer old job, sir, wouldn't you say?'

Gently had his pipe on, and merely grunted.

'I mean, sir, if we have to charge a bloke who's already been topped. Nothing like that on record before, so I'm just wondering how we go about it.'

'This isn't a joke!'

'Oh no, sir. But I can see there may be problems. Especially if you've seen his PM notes, like you told Canning, and him still riding horses and eating hot dinners.'

Gently growled into his pipe: 'As far as the press goes, he's Neil Macready. And you'll be back pounding a beat if they ever hear of an Eric Cleeve.'

'But—between ourselves, sir?'

'You can guess the rest. This is a very hot potato.'

'Will it ever come to a case, sir?'

'If we can prove to the hilt that a Neil Macready shot Judge Pewsey.'

'I see, sir.'

Pypard watched the scenery for a while. Then he turned to stare hard at the Granada following behind.

Gently said: 'I want Stoke and Mrs Pewsey brought in. You can tell them it's to amend their statements. I want them held together in an interview room.'

At once Pypard's face was solemn.

'She'll create, sir. Like a bastard.'

'I will take responsibility. But I want them present in the Police Station.'

'Well . . . if you say so, sir.'

After that, Pypard stayed very quiet indeed.

11

'Is this your passport?'

'Damn right it is.'

'It gives the place of birth as Montreal. With that information the Canadian authorities will be able to trace the death certificate of the real Neil Henry Macready.'

'Only he's sitting here, alive and well.'

'That isn't the tale your fingerprints are telling us.'

'Quit conning. They're not telling you anything, because you don't have them on record here.'

'You happen to be wrong.'

'Pull the other one. And just give my embassy a ring. They'll vouch for me, right down the line: Neil Macready, Canadian citizen.'

It was his confidence that Gently found surprising: you might have thought that Cleeve was playing a game. Tidied up now, his spruceness restored, he looked oddly relaxed as he sat parrying questions. He had given them his dabs with only nominal reluctance, apparently gambling still on the destruction of the originals, and had turned out his pockets promptly when asked, to reveal the personal possessions of a man of affluence. Along with them was a photograph of his wife and children, she a good-looking blonde with a lithe figure, and another of a ranch-style house and a paddock, over the rails of which horses were peering. His wallet was well lined and contained an American Express card and a first-class return air ticket. Cleeve, as Macready, had made a good life; and he seemed perfectly assured that it wasn't in jeopardy.

'Let me tell you something. After execution, the fingerprint record of a man is normally destroyed. But in the case of Eric

Cleeve it was retained in an unofficial collection in Scotland Yard.'

'So what's that to me? I haven't been hung.'

'Your prints and his exactly match.'

Cleeve shook his head. 'I hear you tell me. But I still don't see why you're getting excited. Suppose this man Cleeve wasn't hung, he can't be tried twice for the same crime, and if he could it was eighteen years ago and there's a statute of limitation operating. So what's it to Neil Henry Macready, even if his fingerprints matched Crippen's?'

'It means that you cannot deny being Cleeve.'

'I can deny it. And I do.'

'But your denial will not be accepted.'

'When you're through with the con, just ring my embassy.'

'We shall certainly do that. You entered Canada irregularly and took the identity of another man.'

'So what again? After eighteen years, nobody over there would blink an eyelash.'

'Then why not admit that you are Cleeve?'

'For the simple reason that I'm Macready.'

Still it was like a game of poker, played across the desk in Pypard's office. The brown eyes were alert, almost amused, and giving utterly nothing away. It was easy to see why his accent had puzzled people; at the moment it was practically vestigial. Yet earlier, under the stress of arrest, the accent had been quite strong. Was it something he had under control? Pypard at least had no doubts. Cleeve was the man who had made the two phone calls, who knew too much: Cleeve was chummie.

'As far as we are concerned, you are Cleeve, a man sentenced to death by Judge Pewsey.'

'Come to think of it, I may have heard of that guy through my former boss, Alex Mathieson.'

'The man with whom you flew to Canada.'

'Just the man who gave me a start in insurance. Well, he was often over here on visits to his brother, who was a governor at one of your jails. And the brother had the job of hanging this Cleeve, and Alex was over here at the time.'

'Your memory seems to be improving.'

'Why not? Alex was full of it when he came back. Told me how his brother was sure Cleeve was innocent, and that the real killer was a creep called Henfield. Would that be right?'

'You would know best.'

'Poor old Alex seemed quite affected. I guess it's bad enough hanging a man anyway, without having it on your conscience that he's innocent. His brother took it hard. The guy swore he was framed, that Henfield had planted the weapon at his flat. Nobody listened, they listened to Henfield. And the judge told the jury to find the guy guilty.'

'The judge being Judge Pewsey.'

'I'll take your word for it. According to Alex, he was all out for hanging. And my guess is that this Cleeve, if he were still around, wouldn't be shedding tears because the judge was shot.'

'Which is also our theory.'

'Only Cleeve was hung.'

'And then you turn up here with identical fingerprints.'

'I hear you say it, and it's a good try. But I'm still Neil Macready from Hamilton, Ontario.'

He had tensed up during that little recital and his voice had taken on a harder tone: he would probably have done better to go on denying all knowledge of his former self. But he couldn't; the message was his innocence, and this at all risks he intended to convey. This it was that had brought him out here, sent him after Pewsey, delayed his departure.

'Eric Cleeve had a fair trial. The sentence was upheld on appeal.'

'The way I heard it he was railroaded, and not the first by a long chalk.'

'The version you heard was sentimentalised.'

'Feller, when they hang you it's beyond sentiment.'

'Judgments are made by due process of law, not founded on the squeamishness of individuals.'

'Are you still saying this guy was guilty?'

'He was found so by his peers.'

'His peers my arse! A set of jack-rabbits who were easy meat for a bloody-minded judge.'

'He was properly tried, convicted and sentenced.'

'Listen, he was framed from here to Christmas—'

'The belief of a prison governor is not evidence.'

'Cleeve was as innocent as you or I!'

Now he was really in danger of losing his cool; his eyes were large and scowling into Gently's. You felt that at any moment he might drop all pretence and argue the case in his proper person. Pypard, who was sitting in, was gazing at Cleeve with open fascination.

'So he was innocent—on a triple hearsay.'

'On nobody's hearsay! He was innocent.'

'On the word of a man who heard it from a man who heard it from a man awaiting the gallows.'

'Do you think you tell lies when you're sitting in a death cell?'

'In the hope of a reprieve, who wouldn't tell lies?'

'But this guy was innocent!'

'Not on the word of a Canadian citizen from Hamilton, Ontario.'

'So on my word!'

'Whose is that?'

'Listen . . . just listen . . . !'

Frustration twisted his blunted features, and his lips gaped over capped teeth. Yet there remained something childish about that face, despite the prematurely greyed hair: the frustration seemed that of an infant who cannot get an adult to understand.

'You are Eric Cleeve, formerly a claims clerk at the Brighton branch of Southern Alliance Assurance.'

'I'm Macready. Ring my embassy. They know damned well who I am.'

'They only know who you say you are.'

'Neil Macready. You try to prove different.'

'A Canadian citizen.'

'Damn right I am.'

'In London to represent your firm at a conference.'

'Now you've got it.'

Gently nodded. 'A Canadian citizen. Going about London on his lawful occasions. So why was he seen leaving a certain summerhouse in Wiltshire, at 2.50 p.m. last Friday?'

'A certain . . . what summerhouse?'

'Said to be in a hurry to reach concealment.'

'But I was never there!'

'You weren't where?'

'There . . . in the place you're talking about.'

'Do I get to a smoke . . . ?'

For a moment he'd been rocking, but then he recovered himself with a jerk. Among the possessions on the desk was the pack of Chesterfields, and he reached out towards them.

'You can smoke.'

He lit a cigarette and inhaled deep lungfuls. The smoke had a coarse fragrance and spread in bands in the puggy air of the office.

'So what's this place, then—this summerhouse?'

'You know that as well as I.'

'If you say so. But on Friday I went for a hike over those hills.'

'On Friday you had lunch at the Cross Keys in Erchildown.'

'It seems to me I cut lunch on Friday.'

'You asked the barmaid the direction of Judge Pewsey's house.'

'This must be about two other fellers.'

They were back again in the poker game and that strange little quirk of confidence was returning. Cigarette going, Cleeve sat with squinting eyes, a parry ready for every thrust.

'You proceeded along the Prior's Compton road, then broke through a fence into the New Place woods. There you stopped to light a cigarette and you discarded the empty pack. The pack matches others in your possession and bears an identical manufacturer's coding.'

'Uhuh.' Cleeve inhaled. 'Only so would a couple of million

others. That's no sweat. Guys smoke Chesterfields even in Wiltshire, U.K.'

'Where you entered the woods bluebells were growing and your track through them shows plainly. You came to the track from the New Place to the summerhouse and you paused there, concealed behind an elder. You were waiting for a certain person.'

'So who would I know there to wait for?'

'The possessor of your fingerprints would know someone.'

'Oh sure.' He kept smoking. 'Now we're back there again.'

'You met them. You received this.' Gently hoisted up the gun. 'And you received your instructions. Then you proceeded to the summerhouse.'

'Hey, hold it. Play fair, feller!' Cleeve's eyes hooked wide. 'Nobody handed me any gun, you can leave that out of the story.'

'Not this gun?'

'Not any gun. Just forget about the hardware.'

'This gun shot Judge Pewsey.'

'But that's a different tale, isn't it?'

'Is it?'

'I'm telling you, feller.' He puffed hard at the cigarette.

'Very well, then. But you went next to the summerhouse.'

'Don't forget that all this is a try-on.'

'There you waited. The time was two-thirty. You were awaiting the arrival of Judge Pewsey.'

'Who told you this yarn?'

'We have facts and testimony.'

'Sure, but the testimony is punk. Somebody got in first is all. They've been stringing you along.'

'They?'

'Whoever put you up to it.'

'Whoever put me up to what?'

'That I was laying for the old cuss with a gun. Just leave it out, that's what I'm saying.'

'Yet you were there.'

'Who says?'

'A piece of evidence that doesn't lie.'

Cleeve stared at Gently for a long moment, then shook his head and exhaled smoke.

'I was out hiking, you remember? No guns, no summer-house, no shooting. If you have got evidence, I'm calling it. Like you might fake some if you had it or not.'

'I'm not faking.'

'So you tell me. But you're a cop like the rest of the breed.'

Gently rose. 'Come with me,' he said.

Cleeve hesitated, eyes cautious. Then he shrugged, stubbed the cigarette, got to his feet and followed Gently.

Gently led him through reception into a passage where there were three doors with observation panels. Gently glanced through the first: seated in the room were Stoke and Mrs Pewsey, he leaning on a table, head in hands, she sitting stiffly, on her face an expression of controlled fury. Also in the picture was a uniform-man, rocking on his heels and gazing at nothing.

'Take a look.'

He shoved Cleeve towards the door. Just at that instant Mrs Pewsey looked up: he heard Cleeve gasp. Cleeve pulled away from the door, stood staring accusingly at Gently.

'So you've got them—you had them all along! You were just trying to pump me back there.'

'We need your testimony. And so perhaps do they.'

'Yeah—yeah.' His eyes were bemused. 'Only it was her who grabbed the gun, did you know that?'

'Then the man took the gun from her.'

'Yes. But how—?'

'Let's go back and talk some more.'

'What I want to know is what they've been saying!'

Back in the office, Cleeve was looking nettled. He had snatched another cigarette without asking permission, then stuffed the pack into his pocket. No more poker! He had blown the gaff, and his manner to Gently was belligerent. Over there in Hamilton, no doubt, he was used to people jumping to his commands.

'I mean, there's a thing called the Fifth Amendment. I don't have to tell you another word.'

'For your sake and theirs I think you had better. We can place you for certain in that summerhouse.'

'That feller was too far off.'

'Then you saw him?'

Resentfully, Cleeve drove smoke through his nose. 'So where do I begin?'

'For a start, I'd want to know why a conference-delegate from London was wandering through the woods at Erchildown New Place.'

'Let's say I love the country.' His tone was sulky. 'I'm touring here and read about that house. So I go to look, get lost in the woods, become worried in case I'm caught trespassing. How does that fit?'

'It would fit Macready. But the fingerprints fit Cleeve.'

'Feller, this is Macready making the statement—that you buy, or I quote the Amendment.'

'Carry on.'

'I run across this track and stand wondering whether to go down to the house. Then I see a lady coming towards me and I decide I had better clear out. I go up the track. The lady is still coming. There's only the one place to hide. I push in behind the summerhouse where it's all grown over with creepers. Then, goddamn it, she unlocks the door and starts laying out a pile of cushions: she's going to stay. And I'm stuck there watching her through a peep-hole in the wall.'

'We are talking about Mrs Pewsey.'

'Right, though I didn't know that then. And about five minutes later comes this guy, the one who's in the cooler with her now. There's some heavy grappling going on. I'm beginning to wonder if I can't sneak away. But suddenly the door flies open and there's this little old guy holding a gun on them.'

'Whom you recognised as Judge Pewsey.'

'Leave it out. I'm saying he was a little old guy with a gun. Maybe now I know it was Judge Pewsey, but right then I didn't know him from Cain. He says: So this is the game, it's true what Mark told me at Easter. She says: Give me that gun, Arthur, and he says: Oh no, my fine lady. Then she jumps him and wrestles for the gun, and the guy with her was pleading with her to lay off, and the little old guy is hanging on like a leech for all he is nowhere near her weight. Then at last she gives one hell of a jerk, and that was when the gun went off. It caught the little guy flush in the chest and bowled him over like a rabbit. Oh God, Angie, you've killed him, the other guy says, and snatches the gun off her. And the little feller was dead all right. I could see him lying there, mouth open, head turned to the side. Feel his pulse, she says, but the other guy won't, so she gets right down and feels it herself, and meanwhile the other guy is carrying on about how they are done for, it'll surely be life. Pull yourself together, she tells him, get back to your car and leave it to me, Arthur was always out with his gun, everyone will take it for an accident. She is the one with the spunk, I can tell you. In the end she drives him out of the summerhouse. Then she takes a look around, piles the cushions again, lays the gun by the body, and vamooses.'

He took a last haul on the butt of his cigarette, then drowned it in Pypard's ashtray. He was talking now in a lowered voice, his eyes remote from Gently's.

'I went in there. He had bled plenty, but mostly it had been soaked up by his vest. His eyes were open a crack, staring at me, but he was limp and there was no pulse. The place reeked of gunsmoke. It had to be an accident, you don't give a gun a heave as you fire it. And that old bird hadn't impressed me too much, busting in there behind a gun. So what the hell? Let it go, let the lady make her play. I never should have been there anyway, and for certain I didn't want trouble. So maybe I gave her a hand, like a couple of things she had forgotten about. Why not? Then I came out, to find some guy staring at me from a pit.'

Gently said: 'It was you who wiped the gun and made certain that the Judge's fingerprints would be on it.'

'Maybe,' Cleeve said. 'So what? That wasn't going to pervert the ends of justice.'

'It makes you an accessory after the fact.'

'But the fact was an accident, like I said.'

'Alternatively, you could be charged with being in a conspiracy to mislead the police.'

'Not if you want this statement in writing.' Cleeve's eyes were smoky for a moment. Then he rocked his shoulders. 'So I'm a bad boy! But I thought the lady deserved better than to stand in a dock. She couldn't have had much fun, the wife of that buster, who had made a career of sending guys to the death cell. Even dead he had got a snarl on his lips, like he was remembering the guys he had put away. He lived by rope law and died by a gun. Someone should write that on his tomb.'

'Cleeve's fingerprint was found on the handle of the door.'

'So maybe his ghost was around there, fixing things.'

'Ghosts don't leave dabs.'

'You decide that, feller. Ghosts of hanged men could act differently.'

'Is there nothing you would like to add?'

Cleeve brooded, then shook his head.

'So now you will write down exactly what you have told me, and sign it, in the presence of this officer.'

'And if I do, does the rap stop there?'

'The rap stops where I say it does.'

The brown eyes stared at him; Cleeve shrugged wearily.

'Oh hell! Give me some paper.'

In the interview room the air was so electric that one could almost hear it crackle. Before Gently could even close the door, Mrs Pewsey was off her chair.

'This is the end! I demand to use a telephone. I intend to sue the police for unlawful detention. We were virtually kidnapped, placed under guard, and detained against our will for two whole hours. Now I wish to talk to the Chief Constable, and after that to my lawyer.'

'Do please sit down again, Mrs Pewsey.'
'I will not sit down. This has gone too far.'
'I think you will want to hear what I have to say.'
'Don't suppose for one moment that I will accept excuses.'
'I have been delayed by a witness.'
'What is that to me?'
'I believe you may find his testimony helpful.'
'That seems unlikely, and it is no excuse.'
'It may help you when you come to amend your statement.'
'But I have no intention of amending it.'
'Before the inquest, I think perhaps you should.'
'Before the inquest?' She checked, her eyes raking his. 'What is this, then? Who is this witness, and what can he possibly have to contribute?'
'A man you wouldn't know, a Canadian tourist. By luck, we were able to run him down. He will give evidence at the inquest that the shooting of your husband was accidental.'
'He will do—what?'
'Give evidence of accident. He was an eye-witness to the incident.'
Her eyes were like marbles. 'But that is impossible.'
'How would you know that, Mrs Pewsey?'
'Because—because! This is some trick. The only possible witness was the man Hinton.'
'Perhaps luckily, that is not the case.'
'I tell you it is.'
'And I ask, how you know that.'
'Not another word—I wish to speak to my lawyer!'
'Don't you think you should first listen to what I have to tell you?'
'Oh, oh!' She would have liked to strike him; her eyes flickered with the light of violence. At the table Stoke watched with frightened gaze; in the presence of the woman, he seemed entirely negated.
'Do sit down, Mrs Pewsey.'
'Why should I? All this is a trick you are trying to play on us.'

'I assure you that the presence of this witness was a piece of good fortune.'

'For you, no doubt. If such a person exists.'

But at last she flung herself back on the chair, to sit glaring her anger at Gently. Gently nodded to the constable, who clicked heels and left, then himself took a seat on the table.

'Now listen—the pair of you! On Friday afternoon this Canadian was roaming in the New Place woods. He was surprised by the appearance of Mrs Pewsey, and concealed himself behind the summerhouse. There, through an aperture in the back of the summerhouse, he was witness to what occurred.'

'Oh, what a tale!' Mrs Pewsey burst out.

'He saw you enter, Mrs Pewsey, and rearrange a pile of cushions. Then he saw Mr Stoke join you, and your situation when your husband arrived.'

'Oh, my goodness,' Stoke groaned.

Mrs Pewsey's face had reddened. She flashed a warning look at Stoke and then a defiant stare at Gently.

'You propose to let him tell these lies at the inquest?'

'The facts entirely support his testimony. He goes on to describe your exchange with your husband and the struggle for the gun, with its fatal consequence. He saw you, Mrs Pewsey, ascertain that the Judge was dead, and heard you decide to leave the incident unreported. His presence is demonstrable. He entered the summerhouse subsequently, and we have found his fingerprint on the door knob.'

'Oh lord, he's got us!' Stoke groaned.

'Leave this to me!' Mrs Pewsey snapped.

'But if the man was there—'

'The fingerprint means nothing. It could have been left there at any time previous.'

Gently said: 'We have traced this man's movements and they exactly correspond with his evidence. Fortunately what that evidence shows is that the shooting was probably accidental.'

'It was!' Stoke exclaimed. 'Believe me it was.'

'Jonathan, be kind enough to keep quiet!'

'But it's no use, Angie, we're sunk.'

Mrs Pewsey fixed Gently with stony eyes.

'Just how much of this evidence do you intend to put in?'

'That depends on yourself, Mrs Pewsey.'

'How do you mean?'

'With full statements from Mr Stoke and yourself, the Canadian's evidence can perhaps be kept to a minimum.'

'But how much is a minimum?'

'It may not be necessary to enter into great detail before the shooting. But your decision not to report cannot very well be excluded.'

'There will be a prosecution?'

'That decision will be local. But what first has to be established is the accidental nature of the shooting.'

The eyes kept thrusting at Gently. It was impossible to read what was going on behind them. Stoke on the other hand was in a tremble to be grasping at the deal Gently was offering. But she didn't hurry. Her long association with the law had taught her to look all round a proposition. And meanwhile her eyes gave nothing away. Except for Stoke's quick breathing, these were moments of silence.

'May I be allowed to consult my lawyer?'

'If he is available at short notice.'

'He will be available.'

'In that case, we shall have no objection.'

'Very well, then.'

So in the end it was to be as simple as that. Mrs Pewsey rose, Gently took her to reception, and the Judge's widow rang her lawyer.

12

An hour later, and it was Gently himself who sat watching Cleeve finish his statement, while a jumpy Pypard attended parallel proceedings going forward in the interview room. Cleeve wrote his neat hand briskly, cigarette-smoke trailing from his nostrils, and underlined his signature with a double flourish before pushing the statement across the desk to Gently.

'So what happens now?'

'We'll see.'

Gently read the statement through. It reproduced exactly the version that Cleeve had given earlier. He had come on the scene, an innocent tourist with an interest in historic houses, by chance had witnessed a fatal accident and decided he had best not get involved. No mention of wiping guns or a hasty change of residence, but they were mere technical matters that would have obstructed the clean line of the story. It was an admirable composition, and in silence Gently countersigned it. Cleeve was watching him narrowly.

'Sure that will do?'

'It will do—from Neil Macready.'

'And that's me, feller. Neil Macready.'

'Now I want a statement from Eric Trevor Cleeve.'

'Oh no.' Cleeve's eyes were determined. 'We had a deal, don't you remember? I give you a written statement and you forget this other nonsense.'

Gently shook his head. 'The deal was with Macready and I'm accepting Macready's statement. But that leaves Cleeve outstanding. And I don't have a deal with Cleeve.'

'Feller, I'm confessing nothing.'

'Between you and me I want the truth.'

'Between you and me—and who else?'

'At the moment we're sitting in this office alone.'

'Yeah.' Cleeve glanced around uneasily. Evening sun was dazzling the office. They could hear a typewriter tatting somewhere and voices from the direction of reception. 'And suppose this office is bugged, huh? Don't tell me it doesn't happen! And like a sucker I go shooting my mouth off and suddenly I don't get back to Hamilton, Ontario. You're asking too much, feller. Once I trusted cops. Once, I trusted a British court of justice.'

Gently said: 'I'm not asking you a favour. I can prove your identity without a confession. But I want the truth. If you don't talk here, we can sit outside in my car.'

'And who's saying that isn't bugged too?'

'Over here, a tape isn't accepted as evidence.'

'That's what you say.'

'If you doubt it, there is a lawyer on the premises and I will ask him to step in here.'

'British lawyers I have had too.' Cleeve ran fingers through his wiry hair. 'Listen, feller. If I talk off the record, at least I get a smooth ride. Or what's in it for me?'

Gently shrugged. 'Then a smooth ride. Perhaps.'

'No perhaps.'

'That's the deal.'

'Yeah,' Cleeve said bitterly. 'That's the deal.' He shook up another cigarette and lit it. 'So I'll act crazy,' he said. 'I'll trust a cop. But not here. And not in your car. We take a little drive out of town. And I get my wallet and loose change back.'

'Your wallet and loose change,' Gently said. 'But not your car keys and passport.'

'And I should trust you,' Cleeve said, scooping up his possessions. 'You're in the right profession, buster.'

They drove out of town. It was mid-evening, with the shadows beginning to grow. Gently took the Prior's Compton road and drifted the Rover along it leisurely. At first Cleeve was silent, his expression sour, his eyes watching the road ahead; but as they left the town behind, little by little his attitude relaxed. He turned his head to watch the downs unfolding, their lines etched hard by late sun, and to take in the yellowing aisles of hawthorn, the groves of cow parsley. At last he sighed softly.

'You know what one misses over there? It's just this, an English spring. In Ontario we have nothing like it.'

'What happens in Ontario?'

'What happens? One day it's snow and frozen earth, then suddenly it's all melting away and everything comes out at once. But nothing you can call spring. Across in Kent I've seen hazel catkins at Christmas. Then it goes on, the snowdrops, the blackthorn, the daffodils, the cherries, the young leaf in every colour, the first butterflies, the birdsong. Feller, you don't know where you're at. This you can't buy with a million dollars. Shakespeare knew. When I come across that speech my eyes dazzle and I can't read it.'

'You were brought up in the country then.'

'My people were farmers. They're probably dead. I drove out there just to see the place, but now it's managed for some company. They've changed it, rooted up hedges, cleared the gorse, felled the copses. I could have wept. I shouldn't have gone back there, just remembered it how it was. I had a brother too, he studied engineering. But what the hell would I have said to him?'

'I can tell you that he is alive and working in the Middle East.'

'Yeah? So now I walk up to him and say, lookee, here's your long-hung brother? It's under the bridge, feller, under all the bridges. You have to get hung only just the once.'

They came to another of the casual lanes that burrowed under its hawthorns towards the downs.

'This'll do,' Cleeve said abruptly. 'Let's turn down here, see where it brings us.'

Gently turned down. Within a few hundred yards they came out on bare downland, scattering rabbits and causing distant sheep to sheer away with indignant baaings.

'Park here, and let's get out.'

At the lane's end was a sunburst of vivid gorse. Cleeve led

them to it; they sat down with the smell of turf and gorse in their nostrils. Cleeve lit up. Gently lit up. For a few moments they just smoked. Then Cleeve lifted his head and bawled at the sheep:

'I'm bloody Cleeve! What do you think of that?'

The sheep weren't saying, they trailed away. The rabbits had vanished into the hedgegrows. That left a lark trilling above them, a flickering speck in the pallid sky. Cleeve looked half-ashamed of himself.

'That's the first time in eighteen years. Guess you wouldn't understand, it's the smell of that gorse, I was suddenly back on Dad's farm. It's bloody ironic, I couldn't stand town living, I was just about to jack in insurance. Then one morning I was asked to step round to the Police Station, and I never walked out of there free again.'

'Try to see it from the police point of view. You added up to the culprit on every count.'

'But I didn't do it, feller. I just didn't!'

'Killing shocks policemen too. And they were under pressure.'

'Oh, sure.' Cleeve's tone was biting. 'And my heart bleeds for those shocked cops. But Pewsey, he wasn't under any pressure, nor were those birds in the appeal court.'

'Pewsey was harsh. The court went by the book.'

'And an innocent man gets chopped just the same. Then all those nice people go home to tea and to kiss the wife and kids. What's justice, feller? What is it? How do they face their wives afterwards?'

'But you could have been guilty, Cleeve.'

'So then that crew is as guilty as me. I'm a killer they're killers. Only they're cold-blooded, and I'm not.'

'You broke the law, they were upholding it.'

'You tell a man that when he sits in the death cell.'

'So you were innocent. But you didn't get hung.'

'Yeah,' Cleeve said. 'I didn't, did I?'

He stabbed his cigarette into the turf and sat some moments staring at the downs. Then he took deliberate lungfuls of the heavy evening scent of the gorse.

'They tried to tell me,' he said.

'Who?'

'The governor, the padre, the doctor. The governor had me in his office with just the other two there. Said how sorry he was I had lost the appeal, said he would bust a gut to get a reprieve. Said either way I wasn't to worry, somehow they would see me through, I had just got to carry on like routine, but not to worry, they would fix it.' He turned large eyes to Gently. 'But how was I going to believe that, feller? Wasn't it, like, what they would tell a man anyway, just to keep him quiet right up to the gallows? Sometimes I believed it, sometimes I didn't, and right deep down I never did. When you're in that cell with those two guys it's like you're watching yourself dead already. You daren't think, you daren't sleep, at times the food won't go past your gullet. When you do sleep you've got to wake up, so you stay awake till they give you a pill. Then you dream, oh God you dream. I've been hung a thousand times. I used to keep feeling my neck, trying to figure which side the knot would be. The guys tried to play cards with me, tell me about themselves, but what's the use, what's the use? There's only one thing matters in there—one thing. The rest's a peep-show.'

'Were you never told what the plan was?'

He shook his head. 'I know now there was a reason for that. One of the warders they couldn't trust, the younger guy, they had to play him along. Problem was on the last morning, when he was supposed to watch me swing. So then I heard I had to put on an act so the governor had an excuse to let him off. An act, feller!' Cleeve shuddered. 'It doesn't need an act when the hangman walks in, when he sizes you up, figures on a bit of paper, goes behind you and grabs your wrists. That wasn't any act I put on. I was certain sure when he went for my wrists. I just went berserk, fought like a cat, kept screaming to God I was an innocent man. I threw up. The warder threw up. The governor hustled him out of the cell. Then they were dragging me along a corridor with me still screaming and trying to lie down. And the whole bloody prison was in an uproar. The guys everywhere were shouting and beating on their doors. Then we came to this door, a little black door, and through that were the gallows with a fat new rope. I wasn't *compos mentis*, feller. They carried me in and down some stairs. And right there below the drop was the mortuary, with a body sewn up in sacks on a slab. They untied me, they dosed me with brandy, they kept telling me it was all right, it was all right.'

Cleeve broke off. He was in a tremble and sweat was misting his face. Savagely he dug out another cigarette, lit it, jammed the match into the turf.

'I still couldn't get it. I thought I must be dead, that now I was going to be laid on the slab. The doctor kept slapping my face and at last he shoved something into my arm. Then I was woozy for a while and everything far away. The governor pumped my hand, said now we had to hurry, there was a plane to catch some place. The thing on the slab bothered me, he said not to worry, it was just a couple of sheep they were going to bury. So then when I was quiet they unlocked a door and outside was a van backed up with its doors open, and they hustled me into this with the help of a guy waiting inside. They closed the doors and we drove away. The guys in the cells were still making a noise, and when we got through the gates there were guys all round us booing and beating on the sides of the van—protesters, the guy with me said, there has been a big demonstration going on.' Cleeve dragged smoke. 'That guy was Alex,' he said. 'Though at the time I didn't know it.'

Gently said: 'Who was driving the van?'

Cleeve shook his head. 'I never saw him. We drove for around twenty minutes, then parked and switched to a car. Meantime I'd changed into clothes they'd provided and Alex had tried to put me in the picture, but for a while I was too goofed up to take very much in. So then he hauled into a lay-by and had me walk up and down for a spell, and after that we sat in the car and got down to the hard briefing. He'd got a passport for me which I had to sign, but first I had to practice a signature.

It was the signature he had faked on the application form along with one from a padre who'd bought insurance from him. His brother had sent him a sample of my writing and he had faked the signature as near as he could, so now I had to learn it and sign it on the passport and remember from now on that I was Macready.' Cleeve checked. 'Do you want to know something? This guy Macready won't backtrack easily. He died in a car crash in the States, and that was where the death certificate was issued. He was a bachelor, his folk had retired and gone to live a long way from Montreal, and Alex knew of him because they were acquainted and not from any announcement in the Montreal papers. So just let it lie, feller. Macready lives on, and proving different would be academic.'

He nostrilled smoke and glanced at Gently. Gently puffed and said nothing.

'So then Alex drove us to London Airport—Heathrow, they call it now—and we caught a flight to Montreal, where his wife was waiting to pick us up. I was Alex's nephew, that was the story. I'd been brought up by my other uncle, in England. I'd gone into insurance, like Alex, and now I'd come over to take a post he had got vacant. You would be surprised how that story went down. Soon Alex introduced me to all his friends, I joined clubs, went around with the lads, was treated by Alex like his own son. I was suddenly a new man, ready-made, the man I've been ever since. I loved Alex. He was better than a father, he gave me my life back twice over.' Cleeve puffed quickly. 'I married Diana, then Alex pushed me into the office at Hamilton. A couple of years back I bought that ranch I had been dreaming about since I first arrived there. I've got a spread, feller, I've got horses. I've got three of the darndest kids you ever saw. I'm Neil H. Macready, a noise around there, a man up the tree and going higher. So then I come back here, Neil H. Macready, international delegate for Great Lakes A., and it's like a dream, it's suddenly all peeling off me, I wake up sweating and wondering who I am. All around me I hear tight English voices dragging me back to some dream I'd forgotten, like they dragged me down that corridor with my wrists tied behind my back. But Cleeve's dead. You'll find his grave. There's just this guy here, Neil Macready.'

'Neil Macready, a Canadian citizen. Who just happened around when Judge Pewsey was shot.'

Cleeve was silent for several moments, and then said sourly: 'Yeah!'

'What exactly were your intentions?'

'When I came, I didn't have any, feller.'

From the stub of his cigarette Cleeve had lit another, and he exhaled smoke with a grimace. The sheep had come back; they lined a barbed-wire fence and gazed at the two men with red-rimmed eyes. Even rabbits had crept out again, emboldened by the intruders' immobility. Meanwhile the sun was sinking into curds of cloud, reddening the hawthorns, enriching the gorse.

'You knew where to look for Pewsey.'

'I didn't even know that buster was still alive. It wasn't till I was waiting dinner in my hotel and picked up a copy of *The Field* magazine. And there he was, staring out at me, in an article on Regency country houses. I guess it seemed like it was meant. Right then, I knew I had to see that guy.'

'To see him why?'

'Oh, what the hell! I didn't intend him any harm. But I wanted him to know that Cleeve was innocent and that he was still alive. Officially, feller, I'm still a killer, tried, condemned and hung. So I wanted him to know, and I wanted him to sweat. Well, I couldn't exactly make an appointment because I had to see Pewsey where there were no witnesses, but the article said that every day you could find him strolling in his woods. So that was it. I took a chance and went strolling there too. Then I came to that track where you could see the house and it seemed like a good place to wait. So then it was the lady who turned up, and the rest was how I told you. I backed off, she came too, and in the end I had to hide.'

'The article didn't say that Pewsey carried a gun.'

'It didn't say his wife was cheating on him, either. But even if I had known I would still have gone looking for him, because why would he take a pot at me?'

'After you had told him who you were, he might.'

'First, I would have to get him to believe it. Second, there weren't going to be any witnesses, and he couldn't have proved a monkey's arse. If he had tried, he would just have looked foolish, perhaps made people think he was losing his marbles.'

Gently said: 'So then you witnessed the incident. You arranged it to look like a suicide. Then you booked out of your hotel. Suppose we take it from there.'

'Where is there to take it?'

'You made two phone calls.'

'Yeah, those calls.' Cleeve wrinkled his eyes. 'I'll let you into a secret. Just about any time at all you could have picked me up outside your Police Station. I was parked across the road most days, where there is free parking and a call-box. When I made that first call I could see your colleague picking up the phone in his office. How about that?'

Gently said nothing. Cleeve puffed a few times and flicked ash.

'So I wanted to see how it worked out,' he said. 'Maybe I wasn't so smart, back there at the summerhouse. Then there was the guy who popped his head up, I had no way of telling how much he had seen. So I staked out in the car park. I saw them bring in the guy for questioning. He was there too long, he was telling them plenty, so I decided it was time to put my spoke in. That was my first call, straight after you arrived and called a conference. I guessed you were the Yard and that had to be bad, because it meant they were figuring they had a homicide. I tailed you out to the house, did you know that? Then I saw you grilling that guy another time. But after that I stayed out of Mazebridge on account of there was too much talent around.'

'But still you stayed on here.'

'So if I did.'

'This morning, you made another call.'

'It gets compulsive,' Cleeve said. He stared at the sheep, his eyes vacant.

'You wanted us to know,' Gently said. 'You wanted the name of Cleeve brought into it. You wanted us to dig up the Cleeve case and believe that Pewsey had it on his conscience.'

'Maybe.'

'That's why you stuck your neck out and tried to make us accept Pewsey's death as a suicide. Why you're still here. Why you're talking to me now, telling me what you meant to tell Pewsey. To someone, you had to tell it. Once you got back here it was too much to live with.'

Cleeve kept staring at the sheep.

'I'd forget it for months on end,' he said. 'It was like something I'd been told about but which had happened to some other person. I was busy, I was successful, had a wonderful life going. The other didn't fit in at all, it was just an old tale from somewhere. Then one night I would wake up screaming. I'd be back there in that corridor. I'd be feeling the rope around my wrists, the hands dragging me along. Damn right I wanted to tell Pewsey, tell anyone to get it out of my brain. I thought I could take England, but I couldn't. Yeah, I wanted you to dig up Cleeve.'

He stubbed the cigarette viciously and hurled the butt at the gorse. Rabbit scuts twinkled and the sheep swerved back from the fence. Cleeve gestured to the sheep.

'You see those woollies? Somewhere there are two buried in one grave, and that's the grave of Eric Cleeve, he's the bones of two sheep in rotten sacking. But he won't lie down, the bastard. He keeps coming back in dreams. But that's all he is, the bones of two sheep, in England's green and pleasant land. So now it's told. Now you know. In the end, the guy I told was a cop. And like as not he'll root up the bones and hold them stinking under my nose. Well, maybe it was worth it, maybe. And maybe one day I'd have told it anyway.'

'Once we had the fingerprint it was a matter of time.'

'That too. There's a joker somewhere.'

'We couldn't not track you down.'

'And here I am. Sealed and delivered.'

'Let's get back.'

'Yeah, let's do that. You'll want to put some wheels in motion.'

Cleeve jumped up: just for an instant he stood staring at the evening downs, the cool line of the tops, majestic in the slanted sun; then he shrugged, strode to the car, got in and slammed the door. Gently followed him, backed and turned, pointed the Rover towards Mazebridge.

Canning was waiting in reception, but Gently shook his head as they entered. He steered Cleeve into Pypard's office and closed the door after them. Cleeve threw himself on a chair. Gently sat behind the desk. On it still lay Cleeve's statement, his passport, his car keys. Gently fingered the statement.

'On Thursday, you will be required to give evidence at the inquest. Should there be subsequent proceedings your evidence will be required there too.'

Cleeve merely hunched and said nothing.

'I could detain you in custody.'

Cleeve raised his head to stare at Gently, then let it sink again.

'Instead, I'm going to give you official instructions to take lodging in Mazebridge, to hold yourself available and to report here each day.'

'That's mighty swell of you.'

Gently rose and crossed to the window and stood looking out with his back to Cleeve. He found himself staring across the forecourt and street at the car park Cleeve had mentioned, now empty of cars. He saw the call-box. It was in use; a man was talking to the instrument in animated bursts. Eventually his eye wandered to the Police Station and, for a moment, met Gently's. Gently said:

'Those are official instructions with which I trust you will comply. What I trust you won't do, while my back is turned, is to pick up your passport and keys from the desk, get in your car, drive to Heathrow and take the next flight to Montreal. Is that understood?'

He heard Cleeve gasp, but then for some seconds there was no sound in the office. Outside, the man had finished his call and come out of the box, to stand uncertainly. Finally, Gently heard the faintest of jingles, and a whisper so soft that he might have mistaken it:

'You sonofabitch!'

Then the creak of the door. And when he turned from the window, he was alone.

He lit his pipe, and read the statement again. A few minutes later, Pypard came in. He was carrying a bunch of statement-papers and his face wore an exasperated expression.

'Look, what the hell do I do with these! Lawyer and all, they've coughed too much. Not her, because she knows her onions. But that bloody Stoke will damn the pair of them.'

'Do they square with Macready's statement?'

'Yes, but that's not the point, is it? Bloody Stoke has written every last thing down here, about their relationship and the rest. If this comes out on Thursday I don't see how we can avoid bringing charges.'

'So have you a shredder in this establishment?'

'A shredder? No, we haven't!'

'Then a box of matches?'

Pypard gazed at him, his fleshy lips gaping.

'You can't mean—?'

'Why not? One way or another, Pewsey died by accident.'

'But—Holy Moses!'

'And while you're at it, you may as well add this one to the others.'

He handed Pypard Cleeve's statement, but the local man could only gibber.

'Then, when you've done that, call Canning, and we'll all go out for a jar.'

13

SHOT JUDGE: ACCIDENT

At an inquest at Mazebridge yesterday into the sudden death of former High Court Judge, Judge Arthur Winthrop Pewsey, a verdict of accidental death was returned.

The body of Judge Pewsey, 78, who died of shot-gun injuries, was found on Friday May 22nd in a summerhouse on his estate. A shot-gun was found near the body.

In reply to a question by the Coroner, Mr T.W. Lacock, Mazebridge C.I.D. Officer Detective Chief Inspector Pypard said that he had carried out experiments with the gun, which had belonged to the Judge. He had found that a small concussion was sufficient to discharge the gun.

In reply to a further question, Chief Inspector Pypard said that, in his opinion, the evidence admitted the theory that, in going to put the gun down, the Judge had let it slip through his fingers, thus causing it to go off.

The Judge's widow, Mrs Angela Harriet Pewsey, testified that her husband had no health or financial worries. She said it was her husband's habit to carry the gun with him when he went walking in the woods.

In giving his verdict, the Coroner said he wished to draw attention to dangers inherent in the use of firearms. This sad case showed how a moment's inattention, even with a man accustomed to handling a gun, could result in tragedy.

He tendered his sympathy to Judge Pewsey's widow and relatives.

And then it was June, and the gorse had faded, and elder had taken the place of hawthorn, and pink-and-white umbels of hogweed stood high beside hedges badged with wild roses. At

Heatherings the martins were feeding their young and the lawn borders were brilliant with snapdragon and lupin, while on the walks the purple-brown acres were already pinking with early bell-heather.

Because the sun was so strong, Gabrielle had placed her tea-table in the shade of their copper beech, and there, on a Saturday afternoon, she sat gossiping with Tanya Capel and Ruth Reymerston. A little apart, Gently and Reymerston sat among the daisies on the lawn; Reymerston had his sketch-book with him and his pencil rustled ceaselessly. He had sketched the ladies at the table, the Dutch gables of the house breaking the sky, and now he was immortalising Gently as he lay, with his pipe, prone on the grass.

Then another car joined those on the sweep and Capel's gawky figure came striding down the lawn. He greeted the ladies, kissed his wife, and was poured a cup of tea by Gabrielle. He brought it across to the two on the grass, folded his great frame and sat. Something sombre in his expression caused Reymerston to remark:

'You're looking tired, old son.'

Capel drank, then lay back on the grass.

'I've just come from a patient,' he said. 'I had to deliver what in effect was a death sentence.' He sighed. 'Ah, me. This mortality is a soulless business. I would never have made a judge in the old days. At least I'm only the bearer of the news.'

'Oh, I don't know,' Reymerston said. He began sketching Capel, his pencil effortlessly casting off lines. 'When you think of it, the judges were in the same boat. It was the jury who decided a man's fate.'

'I still couldn't have pronounced the words,' Capel said.

'But your man would be a certified murderer,' Reymerston said. 'Nothing on your conscience. You'd just be advising him what the law provided in his situation.'

'Then thank heaven that the law has been changed.'

'I wonder,' Reymerston said. 'I wonder. I know it is unfashionable to say so, but it must concentrate your mind wonderfully to know that some deed of yours could bring you to the gallows. I often think that the deterrent quality of hanging has been too lightly dismissed by the reformers.'

'Oh, for Christ's sake,' Capel said. 'No hanging.'

Reymerston's smile as he sketched was mischievous. 'In one sense, hanging is the perfect deterrent. No hanged man has ever yet repeated his crime. Then, too, in these days of recession, hanging has the merit of good housekeeping. It might even become policy to extend its use, in order to cut spending and to relieve overcrowded prisons.'

'You're just making points,' Capel said. 'Hanging was a brutalising, immoral business.'

'Again I'm going to be unfashionable,' Reymerston said. 'I think the immoral angle is pious claptrap. When a man murders, he breaks the primal law without which society would cease to function. He has rejected that law, and cannot claim its protection, and in consequence his execution raises no moral question. It amounts simply to society protecting itself, and immorality stays with the murderer.'

'It amounts to revenge killing,' Capel said. 'And that's immoral.'

'In that case all punishment of criminals would be immoral. Unless you deny society's right to defend itself, you can't dismiss hanging as immoral.'

'Then would you be a hangman?'

Reymerston chuckled. 'Not I. Nor I wouldn't have your job for a million. Nor would I have hanging back again, though I'm damned if I can say why. I can defend it against all objections, functional, economic and moral, yet still I wouldn't have it back. Perhaps it's only a matter of personal squeamishness.'

'Then instinctively you know it to be immoral.'

'I doubt it. I'm a moral sceptic. But lying there like a Socrates among the daisies is a man who ought to have given it some thought. Have you been listening to us, maestro?'

'I've been listening,' Gently said.

'Pro or con?'

'He'll be pro,' Capel said. 'And with his job, so probably would I.'

Gently said: 'I agree with Andy. Hanging *per se* is completely defensible. It is a double deterrent, it saves public funds, and the moral issue is arguable. Yet there is an objection so formidable that one dare not contemplate the return of hanging. It is that, while hanging is still on the book, somewhere, by someone, an error may be made.'

'Ah,' Reymerston said. 'The Timothy Evans syndrome. But tighter restrictions would take care of that. We could order it, for example, so that the only capital cases were those where the deed was directly witnessed.'

Gently said: 'The same objection lies. No restrictions could be devised unsusceptible to error. Where capital cases remain on the book, there capital misjudgements remain possible.'

'But look, you old devil,' Reymerston said. 'It's still on the book for high treason and raping royalty.'

Gently said: 'The same objection lies. We can but get rid of it for them, too.'

'Oh, then I give up,' Reymerston said. 'But you have probably answered my question. No more hanging until God is a judge, and He will probably have a better answer anyway.'

'For me,' Capel said, 'it stays a question of morals. But I'm just a simple country doctor.'

He drank his tea. Reymerston went on sketching. From the table, Gabrielle gave them a hail:

'You men, we have decided to take a stroll. I wish to show Tanya the Green Hairstreak Country. Is it that you are coming too?'

They rose from among the daisies, which insisted on colonising the Heatherings lawn.

'I have also to show the Great Mullein,' Gabrielle said importantly. 'Also there is bugloss, and white stonecrop, and many others.'

So they left by the garden gate and trailed over the Walks to Green Hairstreak Country. Gabrielle was lucky, as always; today, there were not six, but seven little green butterflies.

Brundall, 1982/83